Secrets
of the Square

Including
Super-Short Stories

by

Marjorie R. McNutt

PublishAmerica

Baltimore

First printing

ISBN: 1-4137-1177-4
PUBLISHED BY PUBLISHAMERICA, LLLP
www.publishamerica.com
Baltimore

Printed in the United States of America

ABOUT THE AUTHOR

Marjorie lives with her husband, Jack, on Signal Mountain in Tennessee, just north of Chattanooga. They have three grown, married children and three grandchildren. She began writing as a senior citizen and published her first book, *Fun with Funds,* in 1999.

Since then, she has published two short stories in *One Among Many,* an anthology, and has recently published her short story, *Townhouse Square,* in *America's Best Short Fiction.*

She is well known in her area as a speaker and teacher. Her writing is sprinkled with humor and real-life experiences.

Included with this work are some of her super-short stories.

DEDICATION

This book is dedicated to my friend, editor, and constant encourager, Karen Paul Stone; to my friend of many years who did some of the short-story illustrations, Jean Blair Dolan; and to a local artist who created the book cover and some other illustrations, Carolyn Howard Wright.

INTRODUCTION

When Marjorie McNutt came to me for help in editing a novel, I started with the usual questions—What was her objective? How much work had been done? Who was her audience? Why would that audience be responsive? Finally, I asked what I could do to help the process.

Then I discovered that inside that beautiful lady was a different book ready to leap into life. It wasn't the novel she sought my help with, it was a book filled with helpful information that filled a vital need. I learned that her objective was to entertain and to also help and teach along the way. Her audience was the everyday neighbor who wondered how the rest of the world managed during everyday life. Her audiences were responsive when she provided them with common-sense answers.

With my encouragement, she produced that book first. *Fun with Funds* was a handbook for managing according to God's principles and became an instant success.

Now Marjorie returns to her original goal, to create a work of fiction. The objective is the same—to entertain and inspire. I expect the audience's reception to be equally enthusiastic. Enjoy *Secrets of the Square* and the other stories.

Karen Stone

FOREWORD

I always wanted to write, although I never had any training except for freshman English in college, which was a long time ago.

I'm now a senior citizen. Living a long life has given me plenty to write about, and I enjoy sharing my experiences.

Like many older people, I don't sleep regular hours. If I wake up at night, I get up and go to my computer with my latest idea. If I wake up too early in the morning, I go to my computer then, too.

Out one window, I can see the sunrise and the neighbors beginning to stir, turning on their lights as they begin their day. Out the other window I view the woods that run down the slope, filled with birds, squirrels, rabbits, and many other living creatures, and watch them begin their day. Tall trees provide greenery in summer and colorful leaves in fall. Sometimes, snow covers the land, making it a winter wonderland. It's inspiring, a part of life.

Then I met a delightful young woman in my area who's had experience in writing, editing, and publishing. She became a dear friend, and we have a good time working together.

What do I write about? The simple things of life. Stories are all around me. Mostly, I write fiction, but much of my writing is based on true happenings. Becoming a writer has made a big difference in my life. It gave me a new perspective and rejuvenated me. My characters live in my head and heart.

Marjorie R. McNutt

CONTENTS

CHAPTER ONE
Summer Down South

Vivian unlocked the door of her townhouse. Just before she entered, she stopped to pick up a piece of paper that had blown onto the steps. The people next door were so neat, she didn't allow a single bit of trash to show.

Being the head of a funeral parlor wasn't easy. Vivian worked long and hard, having inherited the business from her father when he died. She was an only child, and her mother lived in a nursing home. Vivian grew up with her father in the business and often went to the office with him. Over time, she developed a gentle, compassionate attitude and often did more than was expected of her.

In her spare time, she visited nursing homes, came to know the patients, encouraged their families, and brought the residents little gifts. Until lately, that was her life.

The phone was ringing as she entered, and she caught it just before the answering machine came on.

"Hi, Honey. How was your day? Never mind. You can tell me when I get there. I'll pick up supper."

"Oh, Carl, I'm beat," Vivian replied. "I just want to kick off my shoes and flop into bed."

"Good idea, but let's eat first. I'm not on call. There have been no muggings or murders in the last few minutes, either. I'm on my way."

The receiver clicked and went dead.

A cop's life was new to Vivian. It was on again, off again, and she never knew what to expect or when it would happen.

She met Carl when he escorted a funeral procession on his motorcycle from her parlor to the gravesite. He was stocky and a bit heavy, but he always had a charming grin, as if he knew a secret, and he looked very professional in his uniform, with a leather holster at his hip. She guessed he was ten years older, and she had just turned thirty-three.

Vivian stepped into the shower and unleashed the knot of hair at the back of her neck. Her thick, brown hair fell free around her shoulders like a shawl.

As she dried off later, she noticed she still had a slim figure—tall with long legs and small breasts. Her skin was taut and shiny, and her long, strong legs came from running. She won many races in her age group over the past few years, but she was slowing down a bit. Running regularly was difficult with her responsibilities at the parlor, and, with Carl in her life, free time was limited.

She slipped on shorts and a T-shirt but remained barefoot. It was late summer and still hot in the evenings.

When the doorbell rang, Carl walked in, grinning and holding a Styrofoam container in one hand and a bottle of wine in the other.

"Guess what?" he asked. "It's Mexican this time. Your eyes were beginning to slant after eating so much Chinese."

Next door, the man of the house entered his townhouse.

Vivian nodded to him, and he waved. With his light-brown skin, dark eyes, and dark hair, he looked part African-American and part Spanish. He was impeccably dressed in a business suit with a white shirt and tie.

"I've seen him somewhere before," Vivian said, stepping inside. "I've also seen his wife and daughter from a distance, but I don't really know them. Occasionally, I see them in their yard. They look like a lovely family, but I've seen him somewhere else, too."

She was very hungry. With wine to relax them both, and an easy-listening station on the radio, they had a lovely dinner. Afterward, they sat outside and watched the sunset. Later, Carl read to her from Wordsworth.

The sun, above mountain's head,
A freshening luster mellow
Through all the long green fields has spread,
His first sweet evening yellow.

They both loved poetry. He read to her until she fell asleep on the sofa. Carl closed the book, picked up the Styrofoam container, and quietly left, closing the door behind him.

To accomplish everything she had to do, Vivian had a fairly rigid routine. Each morning, she rose at six, made coffee, and sat to read her devotional. She also had what she called her *little red book,* which divided Scripture into short daily readings. The book, small enough to carry in her purse, was a modern translation.

She often told her mother, "If I didn't have this, I wouldn't know what to do each day."

Sometimes, she took down her study Bible and read the

same passage and accompanying notes. She gave copies of the little red books to patients in the nursing homes she visited, then discussed verses with them on her visits.

Part of her morning routine was to scan the newspaper and pay particular attention to the obituaries. Next, she ran around the square for thirty minutes. When she returned, she showered, dressed, and ate a light breakfast. Then she was off to work, arriving just before nine. Her day often didn't end until six o'clock.

On that morning, she chose to sit on the small balcony off her bedroom to drink her coffee and read. It was a beautiful early September morning, and the leaves were beginning to fall.

For the first time, she noticed a dog in the fenced yard next door. It was a large, blond animal, probably a golden retriever, and it looked old and tired. Some of its coat was gray.

Sweet dog, Vivian thought, watching it.

"Here, Cubby!" someone called.

The dog walked toward the bowl of fresh food being offered.

The Square was a unique, attractive development with a large square in the center like one might find in Charleston or Savannah and was designed as a park with lovely plants and benches. Surrounding the square were rows of townhouses featuring a variety of bricks, with painted shutters for contrast, and several different floor plans. Off the main road around the square were many trails, circles, and cul-de-sacs.

The entrance was flanked by two stone pillars with a gatehouse in the center. Many of the trees had been saved during construction, so, even though The Square was a fairly new development, it looked homey and well-established.

The townhouse at the far end of the row looked the worst. An elderly German man lived there, whom everyone called Buz, because they couldn't pronounce his full name. His wife died several years earlier, and Buz didn't have the strength or inclination to keep his yard neat. Although he could still drive, he was barely able to walk.

Vivian learned that Buz was a German name pronounced like *booze,* but she wasn't familiar with the rest of the man's name.

He had already run off several housekeepers. Vivian met him one day while she was out running, and she stopped to speak with him as he sat on his porch. She offered to help him, so he said he'd appreciate it if she brought in his mail and newspaper. The mailbox was at the curb, several feet from his door.

He also told her he could still play bridge once a week, which sounded like his only social activity. Vivian began bringing him his newspaper and mail every day. One day, she asked if she could help him shop. After giving her detailed instructions on where to go, he gave her a list of things he wanted each week. Listed at the top was always *two perfect bananas.*

"One should be a little greener than the other," he said. "I'll eat one today and the other tomorrow."

Vivian laughed.

"I love hearing you laugh."

She became quite attached to Buz, although he was often cross and cranky. Finally, one day, he fell. He managed to reach the phone and call Vivian, and she put him in the best nursing home she knew of, the new View II, where her mother lived. Buz hated it and continually called his financial advisor.

Vivian visited Buz once a week. One day, she met Harry from the bank, who seemed very nice and concerned. As they walked down the hall, Vivian said, "I don't mean to be nosy, but does Buz need financial help?"

"Goodness, no! He's well fixed. He just wants to leave it all to his three sons and grandchildren. He sacrificed and denied himself for them, and I'm trying to work things out so he can stay here without transferring all his assets to the nursing home."

Vivian was shocked. As far as she knew, none of Buz's family ever visited him. She heard they weren't on speaking terms. She took one of the little red books she kept in her purse, bought a bouquet of flowers from the gift shop, and returned to place them in Buz's room, finding him asleep.

As she tucked a blanket around him, she noticed his fingernails had a slightly blue tinge. She'd read about that somewhere, but she couldn't remember where. It had been awhile since she was a student, and she never liked chemistry, but she suddenly had the urge to learn more about body chemistry. There were too many deceased people coming to her funeral parlor who had died in their sleep, and their autopsies showed no clear reason for their deaths, plus all came from View II.

As soon as time permitted, Vivian decided to do some research on the subject.

CHAPTER TWO
Indian Summer

It was Indian Summer, and the evenings were cool and beautiful. Carl and Vivian decided to eat outside on the porch, enjoying the chance to watch the neighbors and their activities. One star appeared, and the couple made a wish, reciting the old poem together.

Star light, star bright,
First star I've seen tonight
Wish I may, wish I might,
Have the wish I wish tonight.

"Well?" Carl asked. "What did you wish?"
"It won't come true if I tell."
"Mine will, I'll bet. I wished I could marry you."
Vivian was floored by the sudden proposal. Carl had never married, which was unusual for a man in his forties. He lived alone and seemed very capable and organized. She'd seen his efficiency apartment only once, and it was very clean and neat.

"That's not a question, just a wish," she said. "I don't have to answer that right now, do I?"

"No, but I'd like to know your wish."

"I wished my mother could recover from her stroke."

Carl held her and patted her shoulder in comfort.

For the first time in a long time, the twins appeared. They lived in the townhouse beside Buz, and the fourteen-year-old boys were identical, mischievous, and loved tormenting Buz.

They began throwing rocks at Buz's windows. Vivian had never met their parents, but Carl had come to her house straight from work, still wearing his uniform and carrying his gun. He simply got up and walked down the street.

One glance at the approaching policeman sent the twins running. Carl returned to the porch with that familiar grin.

"Hi, guys," the walker said as the twins approached. "Haven't seen you in a while. How are you?"

"Fine," one said.

"Would you boys like an odd job? I'm doing something for a surprise and need some help."

"Maybe," the other replied.

"Let's sit on the park bench and talk about it. Could you borrow your friend's old pickup some evening?"

"Guess so, but it's not his. It belongs to his uncle, who has a junkyard. It's one of the few that run. There aren't any plates on it."

"We're not old enough to drive, either," the other twin added. "We don't even have learners' permits yet."

"I know, but that would make the surprise even better. No one would ever guess. There's big money in it for you. You wouldn't have to go far."

"Sounds OK. What do we have to do?"

"Just keep this a secret and think it over. I'll be in touch when I know more."

After the conversation ended, the walker went one way, the twins another.

It was Saturday night, and Vivian and Carl were going out to dinner, though they wouldn't be eating Chinese or Mexican. Carl made reservations for them at a fancy place in the city. He was on call and carried his pager, but his weapon remained in the trunk.

He wasn't in uniform, though. Vivian hardly recognized him in a coat and tie. Having steak for dinner was a big change, as was the elegant wine and candlelight.

"Vivian," Carl said, with that old, familiar grin, "I don't know how to propose, but that's what I'm doing. I'd hate to have to take this back." He opened a small velvet box and showed her a sparkling diamond ring. "Would you like to marry me and move in with me, or would you rather have me move into your townhouse? I love you very much."

Her eyes filled with tears. "My townhouse would give us more room." She held out her left hand.

Carl, removing the ring from the box, placed it on her finger; then he walked to her side of the table, kissed her, and sat in his chair again to order.

"It would be strange to have our wedding in the funeral parlor chapel," he said. "How about the chapel at the View II?"

"Yes. I want my mother there. That would be perfect."

When they returned to the car after dinner, Carl noticed his trunk wasn't completely closed. "I must've been so excited when I got out the ring and put my holster in here, I forgot to close the trunk."

He looked inside. "My weapon's missing. I'll have to report

21

this immediately."

They got into the car and drove to police headquarters. On the way home, they stopped by the View II to see Vivian's mother and tell her the good news. Vivian's next-door neighbor met them at the door, and she finally remembered where she'd seen Mr. L before—he owned the two Scenic View nursing homes.

"I've been trying to call you, Vivian," he said. "I'm sorry to have to tell you that your friend, Buz, died a few minutes ago in his sleep."

Vivian fell into Carl's arms and sobbed. "He didn't even have time to make out his will," she said.

After checking on Buz without learning anything about his family, she and Carl went to Vivian's mother's room.

"This is the wonderful man I've been telling you about," Vivian said. "I'm glad you can finally meet him."

Carl noticed a resemblance between the two women. Both had lovely skin and soft, hazel eyes with dark lashes. Vivian's mother had gray hair, but she looked remarkably well for someone in her late sixties. That familiar, charming grin came to his face.

"I'm crazy about your daughter, but I usually carry a gun to keep from losing her," he said.

Vivian's mother smiled back. "So am I, but so far, I haven't had to carry a gun."

They laughed and took an instant liking for each other.

"We're planning to get married," Vivian said. "Here's my ring. Isn't it beautiful?"

"Yes," her mother replied, "and so are you. You sparkle from the inside out. I always hoped you'd meet someone who'd be perfect for you. This must be the one."

Carl hugged the older woman. "I love her very much. I'll

take good care of her."

As they left the View II, they were surprised to see the twins leaving in an old pickup truck. It looked like a teenager was driving.

CHAPTER THREE
Rainy Night

Carl loved garage sales. Not only had he furnished his efficiency apartment with them, he had bought some valuable books and a few genuine antiques, too. Although he had little money, he had very good taste. He was a do-it-yourself kind of man, able to fix almost anything. He loved painting and refinishing things. If he was off duty on Saturday, he made the rounds of garage sales in town.

The sign read, *Estate Sale*, but he knew that could mean almost anything.

"Look at this," he told Vivian, driving on their way to a picnic.

With their wedding coming up, Carl didn't want to miss a chance to buy something they needed. "Let's stop."

"We don't need that much," Vivian said.

They walked among the items offered.

"Look at that rack of suits," Carl said.

"You could get your trousseau," she joked.

"Isn't that for brides?"

"The owner, Mr. Graham, died suddenly," the host informed them. "He left a lot of new, usable clothing."

"I need a suit." Carl chose a new, handsome dark suit and went inside to try it on. When he returned, he asked, "How much?"

The price was very low.

"Sold!" He wore that suit to the wedding, and he and Vivian forever after called that the *dead man's suit*.

They continued toward their picnic. The weather was beautiful, reminding Vivian of the time she and Carl first began dating, sitting on her porch. The lake shimmered in the golden sunlight, and picnic tables were spaced around it under the trees.

The tranquil scene touched Carl's heart. Putting his arms around Vivian, he held her close as she began setting the table, then gave her a long, loving kiss. As a surprise, he produced a bottle of wine and opened it.

"This is a toast to us," he said. "I love you so much, and I can hardly wait for our wedding day."

"I love you, too, Carl, and that day will come soon."

They touched glasses.

The following Monday, Vivian waited for Carl's usual arrival. It poured rain all night and was still raining, and she hoped he was all right driving his motorcycle on the slippery roads. Finally, he arrived, dripping wet and carrying their supper.

"Sit down and tell me about your day," she said, pulling up a chair on the porch, where they decided to eat their Chinese take-out. The porch was sheltered, and, after Carl dried off, it was enjoyable to watch the rain.

"It's been quite a day," Carl said. "I was assigned to a new case." He handed her the evening newspaper.

Vivian took a bite of shrimp and rice and spread out the paper to read it.

Small Car Run Off Road and Down Embankment

Caroline Cooper, a nurse at Scenic View II, was struck on the driver's side of her small car around two o'clock this morning as she returned home from work. The incident occurred at the end of Center Street. She was pronounced dead on arrival at Centerville Hospital.

She is survived by her husband, Tim, and two daughters, Laura and Joan.

"That's our Caroline!" Vivian exclaimed. "I met her at the View II. She was a lovely nurse and was very good to my mother. This is terrible."

"It was hit and run," Carl said. "There's no doubt. The dents in the car indicate an impact before it plunged down the embankment on the curve. It was pouring rain, and the bank was a mudslide. We've been on the case since three this morning, when the car was discovered."

"Then you need to eat and go to bed," Vivian said.

Carl grinned, and a twinkle came to his eye.

At the View II, Caroline had been in charge of the locked room that contained pesticides and cleansers. She unlocked it for the cleaning crew, now called the Cleaning Twins. Those look-alikes were hired by Mr. L to keep the place clean, sterile, and free from bugs or litter.

They'd done a good job so far, even though they were only fourteen. When Caroline checked the room's contents later, she noticed some supplies were missing or lower than they should've been.

My goodness, she thought. *Don't tell me I have to be a detective as well as a nurse.* She kept careful watch, then decided to talk to Mr. L.

The day she talked to Mr. L was the day she died.

She was a natural beauty, with short, casual, silky, blonde hair. Her bright-blue eyes sparkled, and her petite body kept her looking young. She wasn't from the South, but she wanted to go to one of the universities in the Southeast and start pre-med training. That was where she met Tim.

Tim, an English major, planned to go on to earn his master's and PhD degrees. He was two years older than Caroline, and, when they met, it was love at first sight.

She had many suitors, so the challenge of getting a date with her kept Tim busy. Her friendly, outgoing personality and boundless energy made her a delight. She was a cheerleader in high school who never lost her pep. Southerners fascinated her. She considered Tim one of the last Southern gentlemen.

He was from Centerville and had lived in the same house all his life. When he graduated from college, he insisted on marrying Caroline, promising she could continue her education after they married. He also decided to take a teaching job and work on his advanced degrees in the evenings.

Caroline was the most important thing in Tim's life. They made a beautiful couple. Tim was tall, slender, and had dark, wavy hair. Sometimes, he wore a beard. After some resumés were sent out for teaching jobs without success, Tim gave up and took a job with the power company in his hometown.

Caroline was a big hit in Centerville. Having come from a large city up north, she threw herself into every civic organization Centerville offered volunteering at the hospital and helping the cheerleaders after high school.

Then she had two daughters, Laura and Joan, born eighteen months apart. Caroline began a baby-sitting club, where parents took turns helping with each other's children. Soon, she knew almost everyone in town, and Tim was very proud of her.

Because of Tim's education and common sense, he quickly advanced in his new job. He volunteered to teach *English as a Second Language*, and that brought him into contact with Ruth and Mr. L.

When Tim arrived at the funeral parlor, Vivian tried to console him.

"It's my fault!" he sobbed. "How could I have done this? My heart is broken. I'll never survive this! Oh, God, please forgive me." He was hysterical. "I told her she needed more training and a job so we could send our daughters to college. She returned to school and became a nurse and was just starting her new career.

"She worked so hard and had a double job, taking care of home and going to school, then working, too. Why did God let this happen? It's my fault! Laura and Joan don't care about college! All they want is their mother back."

CHAPTER FOUR
Bridge the Gap

Vivian was at her office when the phone rang. It was easier to reach than at home, so she answered on the first ring.

"Vivian? This is Harry at the bank."

Vivian was amazed at how quickly people became on a first-name basis. "Yes? How are you?"

"I'm fine, but there's a problem. Buz was in the process of making out a will, but he didn't finish. As the situation stands, the View II gets everything, and his family gets nothing. He told me he wrote down some notes on a piece of paper. Do you know where that might be?"

"No, but I have a key to his house. I'll go through what's left and see if I can find that for you." Buz had given her the key so she could come and go with groceries without his having to get up.

"Thanks. If you get any information, please let me know." After Harry gave her his number, he hung up.

When Vivian unlocked the door to Buz's home, she had an

eerie feeling and wondered how she'd gotten so involved. His children had apparently taken what they wanted and abandoned the rest. The desk was still there, as was Buz's old, worn chair, some dishes, and a few books, including a Bible. Then there was the old refrigerator that didn't work. Vivian remembered that very well, because she once put perishables in there, and Buz had given her *down in the country.*

Vivian picked up the Bible, which had Buz's wife's name, Hildagard, on it, and opened it. Inside the cover was a piece of paper with shaky handwriting in ink, along with the booklets Vivian had given Buz.

> *I desire that all my worldly goods go to my children and grandchildren, equally divided, so each can have a car, providing they find this note. I have learned that the Bible is true, and I believe it.*
>
> *If they don't discover this note, I direct that my friend, Vivian, use anything left for whatever is needed.*

The date was written above Buz's signature. In the desk drawer, she found an old, crumpled, black-and-white photograph of a tall, lanky young man wearing a baseball cap and sunglasses, leaning against a tree.

When she opened the old, musty refrigerator, she was horrified to find a gun in the meat drawer that looked just like Carl's. She leaned closer to examine it without touching it, then she closed the door, grabbed the note and photograph, and instantly made her exit.

When she returned home, she found Carl on the front porch, waiting for her. "Carl, I think I've found your missing gun. Come. Let me show you."

When they returned to Buz's townhouse, Carl went to the refrigerator. Wearing gloves, he removed the gun and left for the police department.

Vivian, returned home, and called Harry immediately. "Harry, I have some interesting information. I hope you love mysteries. I'll drop by your office on my way to work Monday. See you then."

The following day was recycling day, so Vivian sorted out items left from the previous week. She placed the empty wine bottle into the box for green glass and thought of Carl. She loved him and was delighted by his informal proposal and then the formal one when he presented her the ring.

She found the wadded piece of paper she had picked up from her steps a few days earlier and thought, *The Lord works in mysterious ways. Who knows which way the wind blew that night? Maybe this is from Buz.*

She spread it out and saw someone had written a few words in pencil, *Bridge Center, 201 Seminole Road.*

Vivian had seen that building many times and wondered if that was where Buz played cards. She dropped the piece of paper in her purse with the idea of checking.

As she prepared to leave for work on Monday, she made sure Buz's handwritten statement and photograph were in her purse; then she noticed the wadded piece of paper with the address on it and decided to stop by there on the way to Harry's office.

When she arrived at the metal building, just before entering a tunnel, she saw only one parking place, so she took it. At the door of the center, she was greeted by a friendly, middle-aged woman. Vivian, looking around the room, saw mostly older, probably retired people, including Ruth, Mr. L's wife.

On impulse, Vivian asked, "Did Buz play here?"

"Oh, yes," the hostess replied. "He was an excellent player, but he never followed the rules."

"Is Ruth a regular?"

"Yes. She's been a big help with getting older people settled into her husband's nursing homes. We don't know what we'd do without her. What a shame about Caroline. She played with Ruth until she returned to school and then to work. Did you know her?"

"Yes, I did."

"Please come back to play with us. We have bridge lessons on Monday evenings."

Vivian didn't know a thing about bridge. Her generation didn't play cards like the previous one. She thanked the woman and left, then drove to Harry's office at the bank.

"Since Buz died intestate," Harry said, "we have another problem. Only one son bothered to come, and he told me how to handle the funeral arrangements. That's how I paid you."

"You don't know the half of it." She showed him the note and photograph, and they spent the morning discussing the situation.

Marcus Lopez was born in America to Brazilian parents. His father was of Mexican descent, which gave him his surname, though most people called him Mr. L. With a small inheritance, he started his nursing-home business. His first facility had an excellent reputation and often had a waiting list. He offered a life-care program, where all assets were transferred to the nursing home, and the patient received care for life.

He recently opened his second facility and hoped to someday add assisted living.

His education was in health care, because he'd been told that was the coming business boom in America as the country's population aged and lived longer. He worked hard for his degree, taking jobs as a hospital orderly and night janitor to pay for his tuition. He took special courses in *English as a Second Language* to overcome the mixture of English and Portuguese he originally spoke.

Ruth, his wife, was in his ESL class, taught by Tim. Ruth had a science degree and a minor in Bible studies from Brazil, her native land. She called her husband Marc, because she wanted all the members of her family to have Biblical names, including Hannah, her daughter. Cubby, the family dog, however, was named for the Chicago Cubs, their favorite baseball team.

Vivian thought about her next-door neighbors as she sorted the recycling the following day. She was in the laundry room and could see their backyard as Hannah came out to feed the dog.

Vivian had never seen a more beautiful ten-year-old girl. She had smooth, tan skin, dark but bright eyes, and gorgeous, jet-black hair. Her body was in perfect proportion, just waiting to blossom.

"May I take Cubby for a walk?" Hannah asked.

Vivian assumed the answer was yes, because Hannah hooked a leash to the dog's collar and unfastened the gate. The pair romped down the walkway.

They returned a few minutes later. Vivian saw the lovely girl hook the leash on the bumper of her father's car.

"Dad?" she called, seeing her father run from the house.

"There's an emergency at View II!" He jumped into the car and raced off.

"Daddy! Wait!" Hannah screamed.

Ruth ran outside, shouting, then she ran down the street,

waving her arms. Cubby, dragged behind the car, soon became a bloody mess. Vivian dialed 911 and was quickly put through to Carl.

"Please get on your bike and see if you can catch them before it's too late," she begged.

By the time Carl reached the View II, Cubby was dead, and a path of blood lead from the townhouse to the parking lot.

Ruth and Hannah were hysterical, so Vivian went to comfort them. When Mr. L came home, he was completely devastated, and all three cried together as they embraced.

Vivian insisted they come to her house for refreshments and consolation. Carl arrived and shared in their grief.

"Now I know how it feels to lose a loved one," Mr. L said sadly.

"Me, too," Hannah said.

CHAPTER FIVE
Oktoberfest

The wedding was simple and lovely. Carl wore his *dead man's suit*, and Vivian wore a beautiful cream lace dress. Her mother, who was present, looked charming in pale-blue chiffon, sitting in her wheelchair.

Father Dan performed the service. As he read through the phrase, *until death do us part*, Vivian felt herself shaking, because she knew how precarious a policeman's life was. She also knew God was in control and had brought them together. His plan would be perfect.

The View II chapel was decorated with greenery, fall leaves, and candles in each window. It was the first wedding held there, and champagne and tea sandwiches were served in the reception room. Friends from The Square and Carl's precinct attended.

After a short honeymoon at a bed and breakfast on the nearby lake, the couple returned to Centerville. Since Carl owned very little, the move into the townhouse went smoothly. The items he brought enhanced the décor.

As he unpacked the last items, he said, "Here's a picture of my fantasy mother, Aunt Hilda." He displayed a dog-eared photo of a young flapper with a big smile.

"Let's frame it and set it out," he said after a moment. "I never really knew her. It seems I was with her as a young child, then I was moved to another family for some reason. No one ever said why, and I never asked. All I have is this photo. Someone once told me I lived with Aunt Hilda first because of an emergency. She might be a distant relative.

"All I remember is that I couldn't understand the way my new family talked for a while, but I was only two and learned quickly. I had a happy, secure childhood with two older brothers. I was loved and felt I belonged. I never saw the first family again or heard anything about them. That's why I never mentioned it to you. I never bothered to check my background. The people I called Mom and Dad were my real family.

"This is a picture of Mom," he said, holding up another photograph. "She was a lovely Southern lady named Lena, short for Helena. She taught us family values, manners, and gave us the ambition to make it on our own like Dad did. They're both dead now, but their memories and teachings will always be with me.

"I'd like to frame both of these and set them together. Then we can get a picture of your mother and make a little group of mothers."

Vivian, astonished, agreed to shop for special frames. She sat quietly on the sofa and compared the images of the two lovely ladies. Carl sat beside her with his arm around her, with that familiar grin on his face.

Later that evening, reclining in the bedroom, they watched the extra TV Carl brought with him.

"It's Wednesday Night's Pup!" the announcer said, showing the picture of an energetic black labrador. "Melissa is almost grown, has been spayed, has all her shots, and is ready for a good home. The first person to arrive at the shelter tomorrow may claim her.

"Now, on to the news...."

Suddenly, Carl grinned and showed the twinkle in his eyes. He put his arm around Vivian and turned off the lamp and TV. The rising crescent moon sprinkled moonlight on their bed.

It was wash day again, and Vivian was in the laundry room. To her surprise, she saw Hannah romping outside with a black lab.

"Here, Melissa!" Hannah said. "Get the ball."

Vivian closed the washer and stepped outside. "Didn't I see that dog on TV last night?"

"Yes! Isn't she wonderful?"

Two muddy paws placed themselves on Vivian's shoulders, and Melissa licked her face, wagging her tail and refusing to be still.

"Go!" Hannah said as she threw the ball.

"Welcome," Vivian said to Melissa. Returning to her laundry, she quickly brushed off her shoulders and washed her face and hands.

"What's Oktoberfest?" Vivian asked, eyeing the flyer they just received.

"It's an excuse for a celebration. They'll serve dark beer and lots of German food," Carl explained.

"Such as?"

"Now that I've finally learned to order in Chinese and Mexican, you want German? Whatever happened to turnip greens, grits, black-eyed peas, and corn bread?"

It was true. She never cooked for him, but she didn't know how. Their marriage would be an experiment in cooking.

"They'll serve sauerbraten," Carl said, "bratwurst, knackwurst, Wiener schnitzel, beef rollends, sweet and sour cabbage, and potato pancakes. There will be a band, and some people will dress in native German costumes."

"How do you know all that?" She turned and saw him reading from the flyer.

As they laughed, they decided to attend.

"I love to hear you laugh," Carl said, reminding her of Buz.

"I wish Buz were here," she said. "He would love this."

Oktoberfest was a mixer for the residents of The Square. Carl and Vivian announced their recent marriage, and the group sang "I Love You Truly" as the band played.

Vivian saw a single, middle-aged man in the crowd who seemed alone. He leaned against a tree, watching, and was tall and lanky, wearing a baseball cap and sunglasses. He resembled the man in the photograph she had taken from Buz's house.

Since it was a get-acquainted event, Vivian added more food to her plate and walked toward the man, but he was gone. As the evening progressed, she looked for him, but couldn't find him.

"I'm so sorry," Mr. L said, opening the door for Vivian and Carl, escorted by Father Dan, when they arrived at the View II. "Your mother died in her sleep."

Vivian couldn't believe it. Her tear-stained face was flushed, and her eyes were swollen.

They were led to her mother's room, where Vivian fell across the still form in the bed and sobbed. When she raised her head, she noticed a slight blue tinge to her mother's nails.

"Thank the Lord she was able to attend our wedding," she said sadly. "That was so important. I suppose she died in peace, knowing I'm cared for now. I just saw her yesterday, and she seemed fine. She was a great mother. I'll miss her. No one loves you like your mother."

"I do," Carl said softly.

Vivian went to his arms. "Thanks goodness I have you to help me. I don't think I could handle this at the parlor by myself."

Father Dan conducted the memorial service, and the chapel at View II was packed. Vivian's mother was a strong believer, and the service gave honor to her and the Lord.

Vivian's mother had married her father right out of college. She was astounded when she learned he wanted to be in the funeral business.

"Everyone dies sooner or later," he told her. "Someone needs to take charge of that. I love helping people in times of crisis. We should be able to make a good living and raise a family."

Vivian's mother agreed and supported him in every way she could. At first, she handled the books and worked as the firm's receptionist. She helped plan and sell preplanned funerals, then she acted as hostess at visitations and receptions held after the services in the chapel. She helped arrange flowers in the chapel and at the gravesite, becoming attached to families who lost loved ones and glad that she and her husband could help during their time of grief.

Then Vivian was born. Vivian's mother immediately became a mother and homemaker and loved it. Birthday parties were her specialty. Vivian had pictures of every year. There were beautiful cakes, balloons, and many children, always with

Vivian in the center. She wondered why she never learned to bake like her mother. Perhaps it was because her mother wanted to do things *for* her, not teach her how. After all, Vivian *was* an only child and the focus of her mother's attention.

When her father died suddenly of a heart attack, Vivian's mother was devastated. She worked at the parlor for a while, then turned it over to her daughter. Soon after that, she had her stroke.

Vivian pondered those things as she stored away the home-cooked food friends brought after the funeral.

CHAPTER SIX
Wooded Place

When Buz's townhouse became available, Father Dan moved in. He was an Episcopal priest, but, far from being stuffy, he was the most eligible bachelor on The Square or in town. In his late thirties, he was handsome and was an excellent friend and counselor who'd been sent to Centerville to establish an Episcopal church.

He began by starting Bible study on Wednesday evenings. Vivian attended and found him an excellent Bible teacher, so Carl joined her.

At the end of one of the winding trails just off the square stood a small brown church almost one hundred years old. Originally built for people who camped out or owned cottages in the woods for summer vacations, the area was called Wooded Place.

The city eventually grew out that far, but the church remained deep in the woods. A large bell on the top of the high, pitched roof could be pulled by a long, heavy rope inside the church. Children sometimes rang the bell at the end of services.

In early days, worshippers arrived on bikes, in carriages, and even on horseback.

Currently, the church was used as a meeting place for Father Dan's Bible class and Sunday service. It was a primitive setting, without rest rooms, and the worshippers sat on folding chairs, but the bell soon rang every day at Communion time.

"I would've married there," Vivian said, "but my mother couldn't have come."

She, Carl, and many others enjoyed the church's charm when they went for Communion or Bible study. Extra heating was required in winter, but, in the summer, there was no air-conditioning. Only hand-held funeral-parlor fans, donated by Vivian, served to produce cool breezes. The building had an old piano that hadn't been tuned in years, but one of the ladies of the congregation played when they met, using old-fashioned hymns from songbooks.

"I can't read music," Vivian said, "but I can sing 'The Old Rugged Cross' and 'Beulah Land.'" Each service ended with "Come to the Church in the Wildwood," just like worshippers sang one hundred years earlier. Once, Carl brought his guitar and played "Amazing Grace" with the pianist. It was a joyful place to meet.

The twins attended, sitting behind Laura and Joan. Ruth always made them bring their Bibles. The twins were almost always together, and very few could tell them apart. They rode their bikes to church and left immediately after the service ended.

Mr. L, Ruth, and Hannah never missed a Sunday service or any other church event. Hannah usually sat with her parents.

Father Dan was thankful for such a delightful place to hold services. The building even had a small downstairs area where the children could meet.

"Maybe we could start a Sunday school class there soon," Dan said. "Then all we'd need would be a choir. I'll discuss that with Carl. We could have the piano tuned, and Carl would make a good music director."

In the rear of the church was a basket labeled *Lost and Found,* containing a jacket that looked like it belonged to one of the twins, a child's Bible without a name, and a baseball cap.

"Dan, where'd you find that cap?" Vivian asked.

"Oddly enough, it was in the basement area," Dan replied. "I was checking for a place to hold a future Sunday school class and found it there, along with a dirty blanket and some cans of food. I can't imagine how long it's been there."

I can, Vivian thought. *Buz's son must be living down there. That must be who he is.* She couldn't wait to go home and tell Carl.

Dan often went from door-to-door in the community, announcing a new church being formed. He invited people of all faiths to his Bible class, and he regularly visited nursing homes and hospitals. Soon, he had a class at Scenic View I and II during the day and was known as the nursing homes' pastor. Often, he was called to meet someone's needs or to offer comfort.

It seemed that Dan's only other interest was to fix up his home, which had been sadly neglected by Buz. Vivian offered to help, since she loved cleaning, painting, and choosing furnishings.

Soon, his townhouse was a warm, inviting place for visitors. The second bedroom was a study that Vivian designed from scratch. It contained a large, roll-top desk that held a computer, complete with keyboard and printer, which were totally enclosed when not in use.

The room also had a beautiful leather reclining chair, a lamp, and a business-sized desk with file drawers. On top was a phone and answering machine. A side chair with rollers served the desk and also made an inviting place for visitors to sit.

A large bookshelf with glass doors enclosed many books. The room was a minister's paradise, and Vivian was proud of her decorating skills.

Dan was delighted and very thankful. When the bishop came to town, he was impressed, too.

One of the townhouses in the cul-de-sac was empty, and a young couple moved in and out again after only a short time. The man's company had suddenly been downsized, and he'd lost his job.

One Saturday morning, Vivian noticed a large moving van and a car with three people in it near the vacant townhouse. She was on her morning run. As she passed, she noticed Tim getting out of the car with Laura and Joan. Vivian stopped to greet them.

"I couldn't stand the house anymore," Tim admitted. "It sold right away because Caroline kept it so well. We noticed the vacant condo here when we came for church. The girls and I decided to get it, so here we are."

"Welcome!" Vivian said. "I'm sure you'll like it here. Let me know if I can help. Carl and I live across the square and down a couple of houses."

The twins walked by and immediately noticed the girls. Vivian assumed they were near the same age. The girls were like magnets. The moment they appeared, boys arrived. Vivian thought about Caroline and how she'd miss that moment with her daughters. She was the only deceased connected with the View II that hadn't had blue fingernails.

"Sometime," Tim said with a grin, "I'll have to tell you

about all the casseroles we've received, not to mention cakes, and how much attention the girls are getting. Actually, I didn't know what to do with all that food and had trouble remembering who brought what. Beth is still helping us. She brings food and takes the girls places. I was relieved to find another house and start a new life. If the situation wasn't so serious, it would be amusing."

"I'd love to hear about it," Vivian said, smiling. "You'll have to come over soon and tell us about it. By the way, I can't make casseroles or bake cakes."

She continued her run.

Beth's red Buick was soon seen regularly parked in front of Tim's townhouse, and more food was carried in. Then the Buick appeared in front of Father Dan's, and it was clear that the congregation had a new member.

She must be a lonely lady, Vivian thought. *I must get to know her and invite her over.*

Beth didn't live in The Square, though—not yet.

Tim remembered Beth from their high-school days in Centerville. Beth had majored in home economics and always helped prepare food and arrange flowers for socials. She'd been voted *most likely to succeed.* She married a young man in the Navy, but he was killed in the service.

Beth was committed to helping others who'd lost loved ones or who were simply lonely. She lived alone and participated in many charitable organizations. She took Tim's daughters places, and soon Beth began visiting Tim and Dan regularly.

Vivian stopped by Father Dan's one morning when the red Buick was parked outside. Vivian was pleased to meet Beth, a woman in her mid-thirties who'd been widowed for ten years. Beth had a sunny disposition, was an excellent cook, and was considering opening a catering business from her home. The idea delighted Vivian.

Beth had natural red hair, green eyes, and a slim figure. She, too, loved running, and she and Vivian hit it off immediately, so Vivian invited her and Dan to dinner, then added Tim and Mr. L and Ruth, so Beth would meet more people from The Square.

The dinner party was lots of fun. The local deli supplied cooked pot roast with potatoes and carrots, and Vivian tossed a Caesar salad from a package. The adult beverage for the night was wine, with bakery cookies and coffee for dessert.

Mmmm, Vivian thought. *Cooking like this isn't so difficult.*

After dinner, Carl took out his old guitar, and they sang songs from the sixties and seventies. Vivian was a Patsy Cline fan, so the group sang some of Patsy's songs, too. When she sang "I Fall to Pieces," Vivian thought of Aunt Lucille, who always became unnerved during a crisis. Carl also played some of the hymns from church, which delighted Dan.

"This is just like choir practice," Dan said.

That night saw the beginning of a small choir for their church, with Carl as director.

Everyone enjoyed an evening free from worry about the recent spate of deaths and suspicious characters, making it a refreshing time for all.

CHAPTER SEVEN
Ice Storm

Centerville was nestled between two mountains that were both 2,000 feet above sea level. Although it was a small Southern town, it occasionally felt the touch of big Northern weather, something no one was ever prepared for.

Everyone remembered the ice storm of the seventies, when the entire city was paralyzed for almost seven days. People had no heat, electricity, light, or way to leave their driveways. Taking a step onto the ice-covered ground usually meant sprawling on the ice one second later. Many had no way to heat food.

One day after another such storm, Vivian decided to sit by the sliding-glass doors to the bedroom balcony and view the winter wonderland of the current year. As the sun rose, the world glistened. The power was off again, and Carl was in the shower, hoping he could finish before he ran out of hot water.

Cracks and bangs sounded like thunder occasionally as trees broke under the weight of ice. A small brown bird landed on the balcony rail. Ice hung from the edge of the balcony, glistening in the sun, and the little bird seemed puzzled. Vivian refilled the bird feeder with birdseed, and soon, many birds were eating.

Sometimes chunks of ice melted and fell, striking houses and cars and causing damage. Small icebergs slid off roofs and fell with a loud crash. Vivian glanced toward the local square and saw the fountain that looked like an ice sculpture, glowing and dripping as it melted.

She'd been just a little girl the last time they had such a storm, but she remembered it vividly. Her parents were devastated. Her father had to be at the funeral parlor for emergencies but couldn't leave. Now she was in the same position. Carl would be on emergency call for minor traffic accidents, injuries, and possible deaths.

She thought about Tim, who worked for the power company. He'd probably been up all night working on icy power poles and repairing broken lines, trying to restore power to the city. That meant his girls were home alone.

Vivian picked up the telephone and dialed their number.

"Hello," Laura answered.

"Are you all right?"

"Yes. Dad's been out all night, but we've managed. We have a kerosene heater and some oil lamps. Joan's still in bed to keep warm. I'm glad we're here, not in the big house. Dad gave us warnings and instructions before he left."

"Call me at the parlor or Carl at the precinct if you need us. Be very careful with that heater. Be sure you have plenty of ventilation."

"We will. Thanks. Bye."

The current ice storm wasn't as severe as the previous one, but Vivian was willing to bet such a storm hadn't appeared on Christmas Eve before.

She turned on a battery-powered radio. "Seven thousand

people in our area are without power," the announcer said. "Two fires have been reported due to Christmas trees being knocked over in the dark, and candles igniting them. One elderly woman was pronounced dead on arrival at Centerview Hospital. She apparently stepped outside to see the damage, slipped, and fell. Her name is being withheld until next of kin can be notified."

Carl, emerging from the shower, joined Vivan at the glass door. Together, they read from Luke II in the dim light, concerning Jesus' birth. Then they prayed for those around them who were less fortunate.

"Think we can make it now?" Carl asked. "Snow tires are no good on ice. People around here don't know how to drive under these conditions."

"We'll make it. We have to."

A slight stream of smoke came from a townhouse across the square, but the smoke wasn't coming from a chimney.

"Dear Lord!" Vivian said. "That looks like Tim's place!"

They threw on heavy coats and boots and dashed to the door with their fire extinguisher. Once outside, they walked as quickly and carefully as they could over the ice-covered ground.

Carl picked up a fallen limb and gave it to Vivian to use as a walking stick. By the time they crossed the square, Laura was on the front porch.

"It's out!" she called. "Joan got up, fell over the heater, and caught the bed covers on fire. I used the techniques I learned from Firefighter's Week at school and smothered it."

Vivian and Carl went inside to make sure all was well, then left for work.

The lights and heat were on at the parlor, making it warm and cozy. The first deceased to arrive was the elderly woman with her grieving family.

Dear Lord, Vivian prayed, *please give them peace. That's what we need—peace on earth.*

She endeavored to give the family good will. When she checked the deceased woman's toenails and fingernails, they weren't blue.

Once the power was back on, Carl and Vivian decided to serve Christmas dinner at the downtown shelter at noon. They invited Father Dan, Tim, and his daughters to their home for Christmas supper.

Vivian ordered three chickens cooked on a spit, a large package of frozen homestyle dressing, and a lovely fruitcake from the Kiwanis Club. She made mashed potatoes and boiled frozen green peas, then opened a can of cranberry sauce.

Carl had furnished a foldout server from his former efficiency, and one of their wedding gifts had been an electric food warmer. The spread looked delightful. Vivian set the table with Christmas place mats and stacked the serving dishes on the server.

Even though the power was back on, she lit candles for the dinner table and enjoyed the thought of her first Christmas dinner with her husband, shared with friends. She couldn't have asked for anything more. The table was just the right size for six.

"This is an adult beverage," Carl announced, passing a tray of wine in tall, stemmed glasses to the adults. Then he passed a tray of sparkling Sprite to the girls. "Pretend this is champagne," he told them.

Carl made coffee to go with the fruitcake. Vivian wondered what she'd do if she ever had children and had to make gingerbread and Christmas tree cookies. She'd never baked anything in her life. Father Dan said the blessing, and Tim cried softly at the thought of being without Caroline, from relief that the fire had been taken care of, and out of sheer exhaustion.

Vivian glanced out the window and thought she saw a tall stranger there wearing sunglasses, but he had no baseball cap. Instead, he wore a dark, woven cap pulled low around his ears. Father Dan lived in Buz's house, so, if that were Buz's son, he had no place to go. Vivian pondered that as she served the rest of the dinner.

After they ate, Carl got out his old guitar, and the group sang Christmas carols. He played by ear, and his guitar was leftover from the sixties and his hippie days, when he'd been very idealistic and sang ballads with strong social messages. He had a good voice, and Dan was grateful that Carl agreed to be their choir director.

After the guests left, Vivian sat by the gas-log fire and fell into a pensive mood. She wondered about Caroline's death and the man in the baseball cap. She missed her mother and wondered about the blue fingernails.

Out the window, she watched the twins walk past and briefly eye the home of Laura and Joan. Vivian was puzzled about the twins, too.

Carl sat quietly, thumbing through the Christmas cards they'd received that year.

"I've been thinking," Vivian said. "I'm suspicious. I believe some recent events are connected. Do you think my mother and Buz might've been poisoned? I have to do some research at the library. I feel an investigation is in order."

"Here's the key Mr. Carl asked us about," Laura said when Vivian opened the door. "Miss Ruth asked us about it, too. I found it on Mom's key chain with her other things. I'm sure it's to the supply room at View II. It doesn't fit anything else."

"Thanks." Vivian handed the key to Carl.

Carl picked up the phone and called Mr. L. "I'd like permission to check the supply room at the View II, please."

"Sure. Ruth and I will come with you. You can bring Vivian if you like."

Vivian nodded when Carl told her the news, then she picked up her notebook, filled with notes from her recent library visit, and joined Ruth and Mr. L at his car.

The first thing Vivian noticed when walking into the supply room was a container of ant poison. The label read, *Ant baits. Contains a form of arsenic.*

She referred to her notes. *Arsenic alone is a poison and a carcinogen, but arsenic compounds have been used as medicines for thousands of years.*

It's amazing how something can be both good and bad, she thought.

After a more thorough inspection, Carl tried the key Laura gave him, and it fit the door. He handed it to Mr. L.

"Who else has a key to that door?" Carl asked as they walked toward the car. He was officially working on the case for Buz, Caroline, and Vivian's mother.

"I did, of course. I always unlocked it for the twins, and they relocked it when they finished taking out supplies for cleaning. Caroline was in charge of the supply room. She checked what we had and ordered anything we needed."

"No one else?"

"Well, there's Ruth. She's been a great help in both nursing homes. I don't know what I'd do without her." He hugged his wife, who walked beside him. "Thanks for returning Caroline's key, Carl. As far as I know, there isn't another copy."

Ruth smiled warmly at her husband, feeling she was blessed.

CHAPTER EIGHT
January Thaw

The Sunday after Christmas, the town finally thawed, and Carl and Vivian were having breakfast. They heard the church bell ringing in the distance. Vivian still wore her robe.

"I'll let you go without me today," she said. "This is the first cold I've had in years, and it's gone to my chest."

The phone rang, and Carl answered on the second ring. Vivian watched as his face turned pale.

"Oh, Ned, I'm so sorry. I'll be there as soon as I can. OK. Bye." He hung up and put his head in his hands as he leaned on the table. "Marion's dead," he sobbed. "Ned thinks she killed herself."

Carl often talked about his brothers. Ned was closest to him in age and had been married to Marion for many years. They had two grown children in their twenties, neither of whom was married, who now lived elsewhere.

Marion always seemed high-strung and emotional, but no one knew she'd been depressed—at least, not *that* depressed. Ned attended Carl and Vivian's wedding, though Vivian had never met Marion. They lived in a city two hours' drive north.

Carl began packing and left within the hour. Vivian stayed behind and crawled back into bed, hoping to avoid pneumonia.

Since there weren't many family members left, Ned chose to have Vivian make the burial arrangements in Centerville. Father Dan was asked to perform the memorial. Ned stayed with Carl and Vivian for a few days, and the children came and went. Marion had quit going to church, and no one knew why. Ned ended up attending without her.

When Vivian viewed the body, she saw Marion's nails had a bluish tint. That was the first time she'd seen that on anyone other than those who came from View II.

"How'd she die?" she asked Carl.

"She poisoned herself and died in her sleep."

Vivian scanned the Sunday paper as usual, but she was bundled up in bed, still recuperating from bronchitis. Her eyes suddenly focused on an interesting article entitled, "Twins Win Science Award."

The article told her that the twins had won a chemistry award by working with various poisons and their effect on people. The article identified the boys' parents, school, and town, adding that many poisons could be either good or bad. Arsenic was able to bring on the remission of a rare form of leukemia.

Vivian had never studied chemistry and hated taking it in high school. Suddenly, she became interested. As soon as her health allowed, she went to the local library and located poisons in the reference section.

Arsenic: Leaves no trace in autopsy, but sometimes turns nails and lips a slight blue in death, because it causes a lack of oxygen.

Vivian copied the page into her notebook and left. Then she decided to make a friendly, get-acquainted call on the twins' parents, because she'd never met them. When she arrived, Vivian introduced herself.

"Hello, Vivian," the man at the door said. "I'm William. My wife, Sally, is indisposed at the moment. How can I help you?"

"I just wanted to become better acquainted. I haven't met either of you yet, and I'm your neighbor. I also wanted to congratulate you for having such intelligent boys. I saw they won a science award."

"We don't socialize," he admitted. "My wife's in a wheelchair, and I care for her when I'm not working. Of course, the twins help."

"Who's that?" a female voice called from the rear of the condo.

"A neighbor."

"Let her in."

"Come in." William opened the door wider.

Sally was neatly dressed and well groomed. She wore a pale-green pants suit that matched her green eyes and couldn't have been past her forties.

"I'm in the first stages of MS," she explained. "I mainly stay home, read, watch TV, and correspond via E-mail."

"We're from up north," William said. "It's hard for us to understand what you call Southern hospitality. Back home, we would've considered that an invasion of privacy. We moved here because warm weather was suggested for Sally's health. Father Dan called on us, and we couldn't imagine a preacher coming by to invite us to his church.

"That would never have happened up north in a large city like ours. We haven't been to church, but the twins go every Sunday. They're good boys."

"We want you with us," Vivian said. "Life is to be enjoyed. We have a great time here on The Square."

"We'll see," William said.

"Thanks for stopping by," Sally said.

When Vivian told Carl about her visit, he said, "If anyone can get them out of that house, you can."

Vivian laughed.

"I love to hear you laugh." Carl hugged her, then grinned at her with the familiar twinkle in his eye.

"Look at my ad and see what you think," Mr. L said, approaching Vivian's porch. "I need more help at View II since Caroline's gone."

"I know the feeling. I could surely use more help at the parlor."

"I know. Married life takes time, doesn't it?" He handed her the paper. "Guess who the first person to answer was."

"I have no idea."

"The twins' father. Would you believed he moved down here because of his wife's health, and he's only been able to find odd jobs?"

"Amazing. I just met them a few days ago. They seem very nice, just not very social. His wife has MS."

"His background is in nursing home management. He was in the middle of an additional course when he moved here."

"Perhaps we could share him. I need someone, too, but neither of us needs a full-time employee. He'd make more working for both of us."

"Good idea. Let's approach him."

A meeting was arranged.

Another one of God's wonderful plans, Vivian thought.

Now William will know what true Southern hospitality is about.

William, grateful for the opportunity, realized that God had arranged it in answer to his prayer. Sally often joined William at his new jobs, helping on the computer or with the books.

"See!" Carl remarked. "I told you if anyone could get them out, you could."

CHAPTER NINE
Windy City

Not only could Carl not resist a garage sale, he couldn't pass up a craft fair, either. Living alone for so long, he read a lot about fine art, art history, and was familiar with nonobjective works. Some recent painters used that method, and Carl quickly learned it wasn't to be confused with abstract or modern art.

When he went to Chicago for a police officers' convention and training class, he couldn't resist a craft fair on Saturday afternoon. It was a beautiful March day, and Oak Park was filled with children, their young parents, and people of many nationalities. Carl was amazed when he saw three different sets of twins in double strollers at the fair, and he wondered what it would be like to have children.

He stopped at one booth and had a delightful conversation with a Chicago artist.

"I used to live down south," she told Carl. "People call me Dixie, because I'm from a small town in the South. My last name's Graham." She handed him a card.

Carl remembered that Vivian had a birthday coming up soon, and perhaps a painting of nonobjective works would be a nice surprise for her. Most of their possessions were either hers or his, so a new painting would be theirs. He realized Vivian wouldn't have a clue about such paintings, but he felt she'd appreciate it. It would hang nicely in the blank space above the sofa.

"I suggest this one," Dixie said. "It's colorful, yet soft pastel, and it'll blend nicely over a solid sofa. A piece in a location like that should be large."

Carl arranged to have the painting shipped. Dixie was interested in learning Carl was a policeman, because her husband was killed by a drive-by shooter the preceding year. The assailant was never found.

It wasn't until Carl paid, filled out the shipping label, and left her booth that Dixie realized he was from her hometown.

A siren sounded, and a small, remote-controlled fire engine appeared, accompanied by music and a large, tall man dressed as a dalmatian. The fire engine drove in little circles while the dalmatian danced around, and the speaker gave information on fire fighting and prevention.

That was part of Carl's convention, which was shared with firefighters.

Carl thought back to Tim and his daughters, and the fire they extinguished on Christmas Eve after having received training at school. He wondered if Tim would marry again. It must be difficult raising two girls alone.

The blue-and-white Metro train arrived, and Carl rode it to downtown Chicago. One more day, and he could go home to his beloved Vivian.

Graham, Vivian thought, studying the card that arrived with the lovely painting. *That's the name of the man who owned the dead man's suit.*

She thumbed through her files at the office and found a card indicating that Mr. Graham died in his sleep at the Scenic View II Nursing Home. She wished she'd examined his fingernails. She'd seen that strange phenomenon on her mother, Buz, and Marion. Marion hadn't been at the View II, but she'd taken her own life with poison.

Vivian decided to leave work early and visit the library again. She phoned Carl. "Meet me at the library. I have more research to do. Then we can go home, and you can help me with dinner."

They had invited Tim and the girls to join them. Vivian liked potlucks, because she didn't cook much to begin with. All she did was open an additional can.

When Carl arrived at the library, he was accompanied by an attractive woman about Vivian's age. "Look who I found. This is Dixie, who did our painting. It turns out she's from here, and neither of us knew it."

"Hi, Vivian," Dixie said. "I'm so excited to find someone I know. I'm here to settle my father's estate."

"You must come home with us and see the painting," Vivian said. "You can join our potluck. We have some other guests we'd like you to meet."

"This would never happen in Chicago, at least not where I live," Dixie said. "I'd forgotten how friendly and open the South is. I'd love to join you."

It was settled. Vivian closed her reference book and placed it on the shelf, then all three of them headed for home.

Tim and Dixie hit it off immediately, and the girls liked her, too.

"I love it here," Dixie said, "but I'm afraid I'd be bored if I stayed. Chicago has the Art Institute of Chicago on Michigan Avenue, which has the largest collection of French Impressionists besides the Louvre in Paris. There's also a magnificent aquarium and the Abler Planetarium. I love Grant Park and Buckingham Fountain. Chicago has so many interesting things to do and see.

"I live in the Marina Towers. They're an unusual high-rise with parking on the first few stories, then condos above. I'm on the fifteenth floor, which is great for my art. I can see the whole city from there.

"Often, I walk to a charming little restaurant called the Governor's Pub for meals. You can eat outside under the umbrella and watch the world go by. Fourteen million people live in the greater Chicago area. Can you imagine? Have you ever seen Navy Pier? It's a huge entertainment center that the Navy donated to the city.

"I love the museum of Smith's Stained Glass Windows. The Winter Festival is wonderful. I could go on and on. It's a beautiful city. You can always go sailing on Lake Michigan, provided you have a boat." She laughed.

"I'd love to visit the city," Vivian said. "I've never been there."

"I have," Carl said. "I couldn't wait to get home."

CHAPTER TEN
Springtime in the Square

"Today's the first day of spring," Carl said, eyeing the calendar.

"I know," Vivian said. "Just look at the square! It'll be a beautiful day. The forsythia are bright yellow, and the hostas are coming up."

"Let's take the day off and drive up to see Ned."

"Great idea. I can pack a picnic lunch for us."

Carl called Ned, and it was soon settled. Driving up, Vivian and Carl contemplated recent events. They hadn't seen Ned since the funeral and had almost no contact with him.

"I'll help him clean out Marion's things if he needs help," Vivian said. "I don't know what his children have done. That's a difficult task."

Ned's well-kept yard showed signs of spring. Vivian was impressed with the neatness of the house inside, too. It reminded her of Carl's apartment—neat and orderly. When they grew up together, they apparently shared some traits. She wondered what their mother was like.

"Welcome," Ned said. "I've been lonely. I'm glad to see you."

Not knowing they brought lunch, Ned had prepared soup, which complemented what Vivian brought. Ned also opened a bottle of wine.

It turned out that most of Marion's possessions were already taken care of.

"We had a garage sale with the children's help," Ned explained.

That's a little like Carl, Vivian thought, *though this time, he's selling, not buying.*

"I never had a chance to share this with you, and it might help me to talk about it," Ned said slowly. "After the children left home, Marion became very despondent. I suppose that's the empty-nest syndrome. Maybe I didn't make her life very interesting. After I retired, I was content to stay home and not do much.

"She began going places alone, and she met a man who charmed her. I didn't know about it for a long time, but they took bus tours together with a travel group and occasionally met at other places for lunch. There was no affair, though she enjoyed his company. He made her laugh. He seemed lonely and was interested in her. Apparently, he was a retired man who'd been pretty prosperous.

"Then Marion found out he was married with a family to support, and she immediately broke off the relationship. That left another void in her life. That's when she told me the truth. She soon fell into deep despair.

"I couldn't seem to make her happy or bring her out of her depression. She went to Father Dan for counseling when he was the associate pastor at our church. You didn't know that, did you? She quit going to church, because she said she felt like a hypocrite.

"Anyway, the situation became worse. On the Sunday after Christmas, I found her dead in her bed. I've been in shock ever since."

Vivian and Carl were mesmerized by the story.

"Close up your house and come home with us for a while," Carl said. "It's spring, and there'll be a lot happening on the square."

Ned did.

Vivian was startled by the sound of her doorbell ringing the following Saturday, and she had decided to take the day off. Still in her robe, she was engrossed in a novel by her favorite author.

She was even more surprised when she saw Father Dan on her doorstep. At first, she was frightened. The last time he stopped by unannounced was to report her mother's death. Carl was on call. Was he all right? Perhaps Dan came to see Carl about the church choir.

After greeting Dan, she invited him inside. He reached into his pocket and produced a large manila envelope. "This is for you. We decorated my condo except for the laundry room. Today, when my new dryer came, and Buz's old one was removed, I found this behind it."

Vivian opened one end of the envelope and saw it was filled with cash, most of it in one-hundred-dollar bills.

Shocked beyond words, she took a deep breath. "Why mine?"

"It's not yours, just yours to dispense according to Buz's instructions in the note."

Vivian's knees went weak, and she couldn't move. She'd never seen so much money before. There was nothing written on the envelope.

"I'll talk with you later," Father Dan said. "For now, let's keep this between us." Patting her shoulder, he left.

Should she tell Carl? It was supposed to be a secret, but Vivian wondered why. Did Dan know more about the situation than he said?

She would wait and see. Still in shock, she put the envelope in her cedar chest between some blankets. She didn't even bother to count the money.

When a brick came through her window the following morning, a shiver went up Vivian's spine. It flew through her kitchen window, barely missing her.

She dashed to the kitchen door and opened it, but there was no one in sight. The only people she knew who threw rocks were the twins, and that was just for pranks.

She looked at the brick without touching it. Carl had taught her to be careful of fingerprints. The brick had a rubber band and a note attached that read, *Where is it?*

It was time to tell Carl about the money.

"My God, Vivian! Why on earth didn't you tell me? That's not something you keep from your husband. Besides, it's withholding evidence. You know I'm working on this case. This is inexcusable, and you could be hurt!"

She'd never seen him angry before, but he was clearly furious now. He dumped the envelope onto the bed and began counting the money.

After putting on gloves, he picked up the brick with the note and carefully placed them in a plastic bag. He left for the police station. He didn't even say good-bye.

Summer was Vivian's favorite time of year. She was always glad when it arrived. Although the heat could be extreme at times, it was better than the icy cold of winter.

She put on shorts for the first time that year and gazed out the window at neighbors returning home and pulling up chairs on their porches.

"Guess what?" Carl rushed in, grabbed Vivian, and swung her around.

"I can't imagine, but it must be great," she said.

He grinned at her. "I've gotten a promotion! They either like my work or my wife. It's more money and more responsibility! I'm excited!"

"Congratulations!" She went to the kitchen cabinet and took down a hidden bottle of expensive wine and two fancy, long-stemmed glasses.

Ned had left to check his house. When he returned, Vivian heard his car in the drive and took down a third glass.

"We're having a celebration," she told Ned as he entered the house.

"We sure are." Ned held up a bottle of champagne. "I have something to celebrate, too."

"Tell us first."

"I bought a condo on The Square. It's the small, one-story one in the cul-de-sac. I just went up to locate a real estate agent and put a *For Sale* sign on my house. You can help me decorate the condo. Now what's your news?"

Once he heard, Ned congratulated Carl. They spent the rest of the evening in joyful celebration.

How good the Lord is, Vivian thought. *His plan is perfect.*

CHAPTER ELEVEN
Search and Research

"Vivian?" Harry asked when she answered the phone. "We still have problems. No one can locate the third brother. We know Buz had three boys, but only one showed up, and he's probably still hanging around.

"The oldest is a recluse living south of here. No one's heard from him in a long time. The youngest can't be found. I'll need to hire an attorney or detective to help us learn more about him. He might even be dead.

"Can you meet Father Dan and see if you can touch base with the one who wears the baseball cap and hangs around here? Maybe you can learn something. I'd appreciate it."

"I'll try. I'll be in touch soon. Carl can probably help. He's working on the case, too."

The following morning, before Vivian started her run, she stopped by Father Dan's townhouse. He ushered her into the study she decorated, where she felt very businesslike and comfortable.

"Vivian, there's something I need to tell you," Dan said, pulling up a chair for her. "When I was an assistant in a church a few miles north of here, I ministered to a man in desperate need. His wife had left him, and he had no job. As a pastor, I kept his confidence, and he lived in our church basement for a while to keep from sleeping on the street.

"After I was transferred here to start a new church, I lost track of him. Later, when he showed up, I assumed he was connected to Buz in some way, because he had told me he had a rich father who no longer loved him. I assumed the man was Buz's son, though I wasn't sure. That's why I asked you to keep that money a secret. I certainly didn't intend to put you in any danger. I'm very sorry about what happened."

"I understand, but I told Carl about the money after the brick came through my window."

"After I found the baseball cap, I figured the man was living in the little church basement, but I didn't want to say anything until I was certain," Dan continued.

"I know. I came to the same conclusion. Carl was furious with me for not telling him about the money, because he's working on that case. He took the brick and note to the forensic lab, and the money's in the safe at police headquarters."

"Let's walk to the church. It's still early. If he's staying in the basement, he'll still be there."

The little church looked gloomy as they entered the empty sanctuary in the early morning light. Dan turned on the lights, and they walked down the basement steps. Curled up in the old, dirty blanket lay a man with an empty milk carton beside him and a baseball cap.

He leaped to his feet when he heard them approach, but he didn't speak.

"We need to speak with you," Dan said. "Come with us. We'll get some coffee."

The man, putting on his cap without a word, followed them back to Dan's study. While coffee brewed, the man used the bathroom to clean up a bit. Soon, all three sat in the study with cups of coffee.

"What's your name?" Dan asked.

"Herbert. I'm Buz's son. I have an older brother. I also had a younger one, but I haven't seen him in a long time. I have no idea where he is. For all I know, he might be dead. I don't even remember his name. I'm just hanging around until things are settled, then I'll get on with my life."

"You need some help," Dan said. "Vivian and I are here to offer it. Aren't you the one who stayed in my previous church? We talked then, didn't we?"

"I thought you'd remember, but it was long ago. Nothing has changed for me. I'm just waiting and hoping."

Vivian, completely startled, said nothing, wishing Carl were there.

"How can we find out about your younger brother?" Dan asked.

"I have no idea. I'll try to reach my older brother and see if he can help."

"Can you give us your and your brother's full names?"

The man was unable to provide much information. They finished their coffee, then Dan made breakfast for himself and Herbert, who left to use the shower and change into some of Dan's old clothes.

Vivian began her run. When she returned home, she called Carl and told him what happened, then went to the funeral parlor.

Vivian returned to the library again. That time, she went to the genealogy section. She had carefully written down Herbert's full name and birth date, along with the names of his parents and older brother. She'd been very careful to use the correct German spellings. Knowing she wasn't good at such research, she asked for help from a librarian, then searched diligently.

She found Herbert first, partly because she had his full name and birth date. After some difficulty, she located his older brother, whose first name was Lumas, followed by a German name she couldn't pronounce.

Time passed quickly, because she was very absorbed in her mission. Suddenly, she was startled when she looked at her watch and saw it was past time to be home for supper.

She was about to close the book when she saw the name and birth date of the youngest brother. It was Karl, not Carl, and the birth date was the same as that of her beloved husband!

Vivian stared at the page in shock. Karl's mother's name was Hildagard, the same as her husband's aunt. Was it possible that Carl had two real brothers and two stepbrothers? Perhaps Buz was his father, and Carl didn't even know it.

She was so shocked, she could hardly move.

When she arrived home, Carl asked, "What's wrong, Vivian? You're as white as a ghost. What happened to make you so late?"

Collapsing on the sofa, she took a few deep breaths. Carl sat beside her, looking alarmed.

How could she tell him? Where should she begin? He was the key to the mystery of two families!

She began speaking and continued her tale as they ate supper. After they ate, they dashed to the library to continue their research.

CHAPTER TWELVE
Breeze Through the Door

The party was very special, and the invitation read, *Festival for Newcomers from Brazil*. The card included a date, time, and an RSVP number to call.

When Vivian called, she heard two voices on the answering machine.

"Hello, I'm Ruth. *Eu nao posso atender o telefone.*"

"I'm Marc or Mr. L. I can't answer the phone right now."

"*Por favor deixe seu numero.*"

"Please leave your name and telephone number or a message."

"*Eu ligo voce depois.*"

"I'll call you back."

"*Tchau.*"

"Bye."

Vivian left a message accepting for Carl and herself.

Ruth was ecstatic the day of the party. Several families from Brazil came. Some were related to her. Some were just friends.

There was music, dancing, singing, and chatting in English and Portuguese. Hannah was excited to meet her cousins, friends, and family.

It was a joyful evening. Brazilian food and beverages were plentiful. The crowd overflowed to the backyard, which was adorned with colorful balloons. Melissa joined in the fun with the children. Laura and Joan were there, too.

Carl, Vivian, Tim, and Dixie attended. Dixie had a surprise for everyone—a new engagement ring. Tim had given it to her a few days earlier, and the other women were as thrilled as she.

Tim visualized a new class for *English as a Second Language*. Father Dan made the rounds, meeting guests and inviting them to church, with Ruth translating.

"We speak Portuguese on Monday, Wednesday, and Friday," Ruth commented, "and English on Tuesday, Thursday, and Saturday. Sunday is open. Hannah knows both languages."

Later, the group moved to the square to view the surroundings, and the twins came to meet them.

Carl watched his precious wife mingle with the others at the party. When Vivian was around, she lifted people's spirits. Even though her vocation often involved sadness, her personality and love of others were electrifying. Even now, she was able to win the hearts of some of the Brazilians, even though she didn't speak their language.

It was an evening like nothing Vivian had experienced before. She loved it.

Ruth, born in Brazil to an affluent family, was the middle child of three sisters. She wasn't the eldest, prettiest, or smartest, and neither was she the spoiled, pampered baby. She was just there, with no special distinction. The only thing she did to gain attention and acclaim was to marry first.

She met Mr. L when he was sent to Brazil on a project due to his knowledge of Portuguese; although, since he was born in the States, he wasn't completely fluent. Still, his family spoke it at home occasionally.

He was on a temporary assignment while working toward his training for the nursing-home business, and he met Ruth at a Bible seminar. After a few dates and hearing a lot about America, Ruth knew she wanted Marc and to live in the States.

They had a lovely wedding, with both sisters as maids of honor, then they left for the United States. Mr. L adored Ruth, and she was a perfect helpmate. She loved him dearly.

When Hannah arrived, she became the joy of her parents' lives. They were serious, hard-working people who were determined that their daughter would have the best of everything.

Hannah, a sweet, loving girl, was very beautiful. It seemed Ruth had done something better than her sisters and first, too! She loved her family and hoped they all would experience the wonderful life she enjoyed in America.

The first wedding at the little church was that of Dixie and Tim. Dixie had no children, but Joan and Laura loved her. By the time her father's estate was settled, she had again learned to love the South and her hometown.

She found there was a lot more to do there than she first thought. Previously, she had taught in public schools. Now she began a campaign to bring art, music, and the Bible back into schools, despite the budgets being cut.

Dixie thought of Martin Luther King's words, "Intelligence and character are the goals of true education." To her, that meant the finer things in life, like music, art, and the Bible. She was incensed to find that these important things had been removed from education.

Soon, she found her niche as a volunteer roving teacher in the Centerville schools. It was an extremely rewarding career, and, although there were no paychecks, she was warmly appreciated and still had time to paint and put on art shows. Soon, she learned to say, "Y'all," instead of "You guys."

Dixie's long brown hair was piled on her head with a lace ribbon around it. Her blue eyes sparkled, and she wore an old-fashioned vintage dress, soft, thin, and trimmed with lace. Tim still had his beard and was very handsome in his tuxedo. Joan and Laura were dressed alike in lavender as they led the procession.

Outside the church, a horse-drawn carriage carried the bride and groom to the outdoor reception in the square, with the congregation following through the woods as the church bell sounded in the distance.

Vivian hardly ever locked her doors, because life at The Square was safe and friendly. Besides, she enjoyed having a fresh breeze flowing through the house.

When she heard the screen door close, she assumed Carl was home early from work and called, "Hi."

She turned and saw a tall man wearing a ski mask.

"Where is it?" he demanded.

"What?"

"The money, of course. I know you have it."

"No, I don't. Honest."

"We'll see." He began ransacking the house. Vivian saw the handle of a knife protruding from his back pocket.

After opening a few drawers, the man walked to her cedar chest. He threw out the blankets without finding the money, then he grabbed Vivian as she bolted for the door. He tossed her in the chest and closed the lid, turning the lock.

She heard the key fall to the floor outside, then the man walked away. Being inside the chest made her think of a coffin. She couldn't quite straighten out her legs, and she couldn't turn over.

She began to pray, then she thought, *What if Carl's late coming in? He's late a lot if they have an emergency. Banging on the lid is futile unless someone can hear me.*

Closing her eyes, she lay still.

"Carl, you take this one," the captain said. "It's near your house and won't take long."

Carl got on his motorcycle and drove toward the traffic accident.

Ned decided to take a walk. After he rounded the square, he wandered down one of the winding trails and became absorbed in its beauty. Wildflowers grew everywhere, and the setting sun made a fantastic, shadowy effect.

I wish I were a painter, he thought.

He lost track of time until he finally looked at his watch and realized he had to return home. *Vivian will probably have supper ready, and Carl should be there, too.*

When he opened the screen door, the house was very quiet inside.

"Vivian? Carl?"

There was no answer. Then he heard a faint tapping coming from the bedroom. Seeing the ransacked room, he rushed toward the sound.

Dear Lord! he thought. *Something dreadful has happened.*

He frantically tried to open the cedar chest, but it was

securely locked. He turned to run for a toolbox when he saw the key on the floor and used it to open the chest.

Vivian lay still, almost unconscious. Carl walked in just as Ned lifted her out, and he ran to fetch a cool cloth.

They carefully placed Vivian on the bed, the cloth on her forehead, and tipped her head back so she could sip some ice water. She'd be able to talk in a few minutes. As Carl hugged her, he felt himself shaking.

CHAPTER THIRTEEN
Chilling Thoughts

Doing research was becoming a habit for Vivian. She had gathered more information in the past few weeks than she'd dug up her entire life.

The drive to the adjacent county was lovely. The weather was beautiful for a trip to the area where Carl had been born.

She tried the courthouse first. After a difficult search, she located Herbert's birth record. His parents were Buz and Hildagard. She looked up Carl's current last name, Mangum, which was also hers, but she soon saw that no child named Carl or Karl had been born to anyone with that name.

Next, she went to the local newspaper. "Do you have any way of looking up news from forty-five years ago?"

"If we do," the woman at the desk replied, "it would be on microfiche in the computer room. I'll take you there, and you can try, but we close at five."

Vivian saw it was already three-thirty. Unfamiliar with such equipment, she was very slow using the microfiche reader. She began with Carl's birth date and searched through many pages of old newspaper stories, looking for clues.

At four forty-five, she had finished three years' worth of local news. Then, as she went back closer to Carl's birth, she saw a headline that caught her eye.

Two-Year-Old Boy Kidnapped

Children are vanishing by the hundreds from our state, yet only a fraction of those missing are abducted by strangers. The latest report is of Karl Wolfort Buzzutto, age two, who was taken from a cart in the grocery store while his mother, Hildagard, was selecting canned goods.

"When I turned around," she said, "he had disappeared." She spoke with a distinctive German accent, and the little boy might speak German. That might help others find him. The police have no suspects at this time.

Included with the article was a small photograph of a little boy with a big smile.

As Vivian continued flipping through the pages, she saw another tragic article entitled, "Accident Takes Life of Samuel Lee Mangum." The article explained that this two-year-old child had gotten into some cleaning supplies at home and been poisoned.

Nervously, Vivian decided to check the birth announcements for the day Carl was born. She diligently searched through old newspapers and finally saw a listing for Karl Wolfort Buzzutto.

Below that was also the name, Samuel Lee Mangum. That piqued her interest, and she read carefully. Soon, she felt emotionally drained.

"I'm sorry," the woman at the desk said, "but we're

closing."

As Vivian drove home, she was lost in thought over what she had discovered and written down.

Karl's birth mother, Hildagard, lost her son through kidnapping, Vivian thought. *Samuel's birth mother, Lena, lost hers through accidental poisoning. Could it be that Lena took another child from the grocery store? She may have known they had the same birthday, and both families already had two boys.*

Suppose it was planned. Since Lena moved to a farm in another county, the kidnapping was never discovered. Perhaps only a few knew about the poisoning death. Now both sets of parents are deceased, and the boys were so young, they believed whatever they were told. No wonder Carl couldn't understand his new family! The first family spoke German.

When she returned home, Vivian was exhausted. How could she explain what she had learned to Carl? It would be a very emotional issue. Too unnerved to eat supper, she would wait until she was refreshed before telling him.

"Carl, look at this," Ned said, spreading out a newspaper with the headline, "Longest Yard Sale Gets Longer." "Have you seen or heard of this? It's an annual roadside sale that runs for 450 miles! Let's go. You can buy, and I can sell."

Carl read the article and grinned. "That would be fun. Let's try it. We'll get together and set up a booth for The Square. Anyone can participate. Then we can all go and view what's for sale."

"I don't think I can last 450 miles," Vivian said. "I can hold down the booth and take a short shopping trip."

They decided to attend and spread the word around The Square. Other families had items to sell. Those who were bargain hunters could hardly wait.

That spectacular event also brought Ned's older brother, Max, to town. It was exciting to see him. Vivian had previously met him only briefly at their wedding and at Marion's funeral.

As it turned out, he ran a previously owned store on the side in California. The sale gave him a chance to acquire new merchandise. He loved the South, because it brought back happy memories of his boyhood.

Now a successful lawyer in California, he was tall, handsome, and had slightly graying hair. Vivian was delighted to see him again. He arrived in his RV and slept there. One night, all of them slept in the RV or camped out just to avoid the long drive home.

The event also brought Lumas, Herbert's older brother, to town. He'd been living south of Centerville, far out in the country, doing odd jobs. When Herbert contacted him, he saw the sale as an opportunity to expand his life, so he decided to leave his seclusion and was thrilled to be with his brother again. His depression slowly lifted as he met others and once again felt loved. The people in The Square made him feel welcome.

Vivian felt it was so unreal, she wondered if she'd fallen into a book.

The final evening at the table, she prepared a buffet supper with many different kinds of meats, salads, and vegetables from the deli. Everyone was very impressed and thankful.

She and Carl had neither bought nor sold anything. Mostly, they ran the booth for The Square and had fun taking part in such an unusual event. She couldn't believe how tired she was after four days, though, and couldn't imagine spending nine days at the sale—the time allotted for the following year.

"It's lunchtime," Max said, entering Vivian's kitchen door.
"I know. Come in, and I'll rustle up some grub."

"I *am* in. I'm taking you to lunch. Grab your hat or jacket. Let's go."

They went to the best restaurant in town and ordered full meals.

"I've been wanting to speak with you," Vivian said. "I need your help." She told him the story she'd been unraveling for the past few months. When she ended, she asked, "Now what do I do?"

By that time, they were finishing dessert and coffee.

"Vivian, I haven't been a lawyer all these years for nothing," Max said. "I'll help you. I'll come back anytime you need me. I love the South and have again learned to love my family and to be near my hometown. You have definitely enhanced the situation. Carl's a lucky guy."

Vivian blushed.

"Then, there is the telephone and the E-mail. I'm now your official attorney."

Vivian felt relieved. As they stood to leave, she hugged him.

CHAPTER FOURTEEN
Snowflakes and Surprises

After Carl's promotion, he worked twice as hard and wasn't home as often. Vivian had help at the parlor from William, which gave her more time at home. She helped Ned with his condo and read a lot, feeling she needed a rest.

She needed a project and began reading cookbooks, trying out new recipes. Carl was astounded. He was always polite about her surprises, though he still preferred turnip green, grits, black-eyed peas, and corn bread. She even made a pecan pie for him, and that was very unlike her, and she ate half of it before Carl came home.

Months passed slowly. Vivian knew Carl was working hard on the View II case, but he didn't say much about it. Perhaps that was because her mother was involved.

One morning, Vivian watched with horror from her window as two police cars stopped next door. She walked onto her porch in time to see Ruth being led to the car by Carl. Hannah and Mr. L stood arm-in-arm, tears running down their faces.

"You're under arrest for the murder of Buz and Vivian's mother," Carl said, "and for instigating the murder of Caroline." He read her rights and formally stated her full name.

Melissa jumped on Ruth, placed two muddy paws on her shoulders, and licked.

"I was simply showing mercy," Ruth argued. "It was no problem to mix something tasteless with their food. They didn't suffer. They wanted to go on and meet their maker. I did it for my people. The more money our nursing homes make, the more of my family I can bring from Brazil.

"I met plenty of people at the bridge center who were lonely, needed a place to go, and wanted to die. I see no crime in that. Caroline discovered my secret, so the twins helped me deal with that. That helped the twins."

Shocked, Vivian watched as the twins were ushered into the second patrol car. An officer read their rights to them, then arrested them for using a borrowed pickup to shove Caroline's car off the road.

Vivian saw Tim, Dixie, Joan, and Laura also watching from across the square. For the first time, William and Sally, the twins' parents, were on the square, too.

"Mom was sick, and we needed the money," one twin said. "Our dad didn't have a regular job."

"We were about to lose our condo," the other added. "Miss Ruth gave us a chance to help out."

Vivian listened as the twins' full names were spoken by the arresting officers. It was the first time she had ever heard them. They were always just "the twins."

"My dad and I never got along," Herbert said, still wearing sunglasses. For the first time, he wore his cap the right way, with the brim in front. "I didn't think he'd leave me anything, so I was prepared to take the matter into my own hands. It's rightfully mine and my brothers', you know. I was just lucky enough to find that gun in the open trunk. I didn't know anyone else had a key to Dad's condo. I threw the brick and put Vivian in the cedar chest to frighten her. I knew she had the money."

They read Herbert his rights, then charged him with theft and assault. Carl pronounced his German name very well, placing Herbert into the car with the twins.

There was no word on the proceedings, although Vivian visited the suspects often. Ruth and Buz's son, Herbert, were incarcerated, awaiting trial. The twins were in a juvenile correction facility just outside town. Since they acted on Ruth's orders, that changed the case against them, and they were also underage. Vivian learned the twins would probably go to family court, then see a psychologist. She and Father Dan, trying to encourage them, shared booklets and Bible verses with them.

As winter approached, Vivian sat inside and looked out her glass doors while drinking coffee. Carl was in the shower. It was amazing how quickly time had passed. She'd been married for over one year.

As she watched, she saw Hannah romping with Melissa in the backyard. She knew they missed Ruth. She saw Tim leave for work, knowing that Dixie was inside, helping Laura and Joan prepare for school.

She could barely see the condo that had belonged to Buz, but she knew that Father Dan was probably in his study, preparing a sermon. Vivian would never be able to buy bananas again without feeling tears prick her eyes. She wondered how Sally was managing now that the twins were away, and William was working. Sometimes, Beth called on them and brought them food.

Vivian thought about Ned's being without Marion. The new condo should give him a new life with friends and family.

At that moment, Beth's red Buick arrived in front of Ned's condo. Beth emerged carrying a covered dish. With the morning sun on her red hair, she was a very colorful character, and her hair color almost matched her car.

Vivian was accustomed to thinking about death, but now, she had to think about life. She had to figure out what to do with the money she was responsible for disbursing. It was an enormous problem, especially with Carl involved. There would probably be attorneys, detectives, and others in the case.

She was thankful she had Max's help. The 450-mile yard sale brought them together, even Lumas, Herbert's older brother. The search for both younger brothers culminated in one person—Carl.

What a family tree, she thought.

Then she wondered how the trials would come out for Ruth, Herbert, and the twins.

When she thought about life, she wondered most of all how she and Carl would adjust to the new life ahead when she gave birth to their first child in a few months. She wished her mother could be here for the blessed event. Vivian missed her terribly.

Carl joined her at the glass door as the first snowflakes of the season fell. When he spoke, Vivian wondered if he'd been reading her mind.

"It's sure to be a boy," Carl said. "Boys run in *both* my families."

"But if it's a girl, I'll name her Lena Hilda, because they started the whole thing."

Carl laughed. "I have a request. Could we have turnip greens, ham, black-eyed peas, and corn bread tonight?"

Vivian laughed.

"I love to hear you laugh." Carl hugged her and sat beside her.

As snow covered the ground, they began their devotional.

Super-Short
STORIES

This collection of short stories is taken from real life. The only connection they have with each other is that they all take place in January.

CONTENTS

Avallon

There's a house in the woods on a lake, at the end of a dead-end gravel road, far in the country. To my knowledge, there's no other house like it anywhere. It's almost indescribable. Calling it original, unconventional, rustic, or different still wouldn't be the right word.

All who visit the house love it, but it's like some cities people visit, when they say, "I loved my visit, but I wouldn't want to live there."

As you enter the gate, which is left open if you're expected, you'll see many sculptures of various sizes, shapes, and meanings on both sides of the driveway.

Next, you pass a vegetable garden with a huge scarecrow dressed in a red bathrobe, holding two lightweight aluminum pans to rattle in the wind. Wildflowers, bulbs in bloom, and flowering shrubs are abundant everywhere. There's an old, restored boat on the lake, and a painted swing the owner found discarded at the side of the road, amid the flowers.

All that is surrounded by nine acres of woods. Perhaps you'd call it charming, depending on your taste.

You might also be met by two large dogs, one black, one tan, that bark at first, then wag their tails to greet you. This may not be so charming.

In 1980, a young woman told herself, *Get a life.* She shivered in an old trailer set up down the road a short distance from where the house was being built. She was stranded, without heat and water during an ice storm. She had no money or transportation and was alone. She also had no phone, so she hardly knew which problem to work on first.

She'd been waiting for someone to return and take care of her, but that time had passed, and she'd had enough. Christmas came and went, and it was the end of January.

With the help of a friend, she abandoned the trailer and managed to find an apartment in a nearby town, then enrolled in college. That took some work, but she found a part-time job and grant and slowly began to get a life.

She was born in 1960, and was barely twenty when she began college. By coincidence or God's plan, her art professor was also a sixties person in lifestyle, though he was older. His interest in pottery charmed her, and she liked his neat, graying ponytail.

He also watched the same house being built, board by board, and he vowed to someday live there.

One of the unique things about the house was its ramps, because it was being built for someone in a wheelchair. It had low ceilings, and the cabinets were easy to reach for a paraplegic. The only high ceiling was in the front, where open beams and glass windows gave light and wall space. The rooms were not carefully defined.

It was possible to reach the loft by climbing a heavy wooden ladder and ducking. Up there was a hideaway where children could play or sleep, but adults were too tall to stand. However, the master area had an attic-like ceiling that provided headroom.

As time passed, the house was completed, including a large porch that connected to the ramps and overlooked the lake. The young woman finished two years of college and changed schools to finish her degree in fine arts.

The professor always remembered her. He stopped by to visit her on his way to see his parents. It soon became apparent that their relationship was more than mere friendship.

Shortly after the woman graduated, the house they loved was offered for sale. Was that another coincidence, or was it God's plan?

One day, the young woman's mother received a call from her daughter.

"By the way, the professor and I are married. We're moving into the house we love."

They named it Avallon, meaning *a paradise.*

Now the undefined rooms are art studios filled with paintings and pottery. Added to the back is a room for a potter's wheel and kiln.

Avallon hosts two parties each year. The first is in the spring when all the flowers are blooming. People of all ages and lifestyles come to view the artwork, eat dinner, camp, swim, and fish.

The other party is in the fall, when golden and red leaves garnish the surroundings. Then, too, people eat, wander through the woods, and enjoy a huge bonfire. Children and dogs are both welcome.

Both members of the couple got a life—a paradise, calling it Avallon with two L's for emphasis.

The only time life is a bit dull there is January.

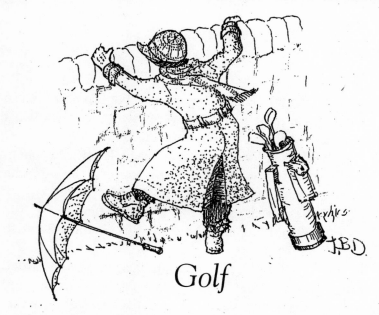

Golf

If I'd taken up golf as a young woman or even as a middle-aged adult, maybe I'd think differently. However, I waited until I was in my midfifties, when my husband was ready to retire.

In 1985, he and his business and golf cronies planned a wonderful trip for three couples to see Scotland. The other two wives were also beginning golfers. All tee times were reserved six months in advance at some of the most prestigious courses in Scotland.

What an exciting time we had! Our first attempt was at St. Andrews, where it was pouring rain and extremely cold. Although it was May, it felt like January. As we teed off, I wore a raincoat with a zip-in lining, ear muffs, hat, and gloves, and I carried a golf umbrella.

When we reached the second hole, I saw the warm, cozy hotel. We'd been told no ladies were allowed in the clubhouse, so I knew that wasn't an option. I'd been led to believe that golf was fun, but that was clearly untrue.

"I'm miserable," I told my husband. "I'm going in."

Immediately, the others handed me things to take back for them. No carts were allowed on the course, so I had to carry everything.

I saw the hotel through the driving rain, but I couldn't figure out how to reach it. Scotland is covered with little rock walls that range in size from two to five feet tall.

As I gathered everyone's excess baggage, I noticed a young, redheaded Scotsman who didn't seem to mind the rain, the wind, or the unmanicured course.

"How can I get back to the hotel?" I asked him.

"Over the wall, Madame," he replied in his thick Scottish brogue.

The wall was five feet high—my height. I carefully lifted and dropped over all the items I was carrying, including my clubs, then placed my booted feet on some jutting rocks, climbed to the top, and jumped.

I found myself in an English country garden, facing the dining room that had a glass wall. I was mortified to see a group of diners staring at me.

I carefully gathered my belongings, walked to the kitchen door, and entered, surprising the cooks and waiters. Dripping and drooping, loaded down with gear, I passed through the dining room and into the corridor to the elevators.

Much to my surprise, the sun came out, and our husbands finished the game. It was delightful to celebrate in the warm, cozy lounge and later enjoy a delicious dinner in the dining room. We looked out at the English country garden, but no one came over the wall.

I'm now in my seventies. Although I've never been certain golf was for me, I played for several years at our home club. I never climbed another wall or played in the rain again. Golf is a four-letter word, but so is love, and people play for the love of the game, win or lose, rain or shine.

Just don't play in January.

Joyce

The summer Joyce died was extremely hard on me. She'd been my best friend since the fourth grade. She didn't die in the summer, though. It was January when it happened, but I lost her in summer. That was when I lost her sweet voice on the phone, her friendly advice, and her delightful laugh.

She was the prettiest little girl I ever saw. She and I were the same size and age, but she had long, blonde hair, and mine was short and brown. My birthday was in late December. Hers was in January.

We became fast friends, defending each other against the usual problems that arose in fourth grade, and we shared secrets. Both of us were the oldest child in our families. She had a much younger baby sister, as I did. Later, we both had baby brothers.

She lived in the country and had to ride the school bus every day, which kept her from having a soda at the drugstore. Most of us rode our bikes or walked to school.

Joyce spent a lot of time at my house. She came home with me, and we spent the afternoons playing in the woods and climbing trees. We climbed as high as we could, then carved our initials. Then the neighborhood boys climbed the same tree and tried to carve their initials higher. In the end, we won.

Bill lived behind me on the next block. When he was old enough, he worked a paper route and tossed our newspaper to us. He always kept an eye out for Joyce. I think he loved her from that day on. He was one grade ahead of us, making him more intriguing.

World War II began in December, 1941. My father signed up as a flight trainer in the Air Force, which took us away from our Alabama home until the war ended in 1945. It also took me away from Joyce. We wrote, occasionally, but, when I returned home, it was as if we'd never been apart.

I lived with her in the country for a few months until my family was settled, and I rode the school bus with her. By that time, she was dating Bill, who could drive, so we double-dated a lot.

Joyce's father was very strict with his beautiful daughter. She was at the Baptist church every Sunday night for the BYPU, and it was amazing how attendance of boys increased in that youth group.

Both of us were cheerleaders and graduated from high school together. She introduced me to Jack. One year after our graduation, she married Bill, and I married Jack. We participated in each other's weddings.

When we started having children, Joyce had two girls and a boy, and I had two boys and a girl. Then she had another boy, and I quit.

My husband's career took us from Alabama for many years, but Joyce and I kept in touch, mostly by phone. We still shared secrets and gave each other advice about raising children. As couples, we visited each other a few times. Then our children grew up and began marrying, and that brought us together again.

Then one day, I received a long-distance call from the hospital in Birmingham, Alabama. Joyce was very ill. I made many trips from Chattanooga to Birmingham that summer.

That was when I felt I lost her, and the heaviness of my heart was almost overwhelming. She lost her beautiful blonde hair, but she retained her sweet disposition.

She died quietly at home with Bill sitting beside her. I still want to call her and tell her about my struggles and joys. She'd know just what to say.

The church where her funeral was held was packed. I sat in the front row with the family, my husband's arm around me. What a waste to think of such a beautiful life gone.

Bill, his four grown children, and all the little grandchildren were on my right. It was January, just past Joyce's birthday. As far as I know, I was the only one who sobbed uncontrollably.

Home Again

I have never liked the month of January. Usually, our mountain is lush, green, and beautiful, but in January, it rains, snows occasionally, and the bushes and trees are brown, like dead sticks. The fog is so thick, I can't always see my mailbox. All the Christmas glitter is gone, and nothing is happening. It can be very dull.

A few years ago, we decided to take a vacation in January. We tried Amelia Island, but we soon ran out of money and returned home early. Once, we went early to Savannah and spent Christmas there. I felt so bad about the people who had to work when they wanted to be home with their families that my trip was a little disappointing.

Then we rented a friend's condo on the beach at San Destin and really enjoyed that, staying longer than any previous vacation. The snowbirds were there, mostly from Canada, and there were plenty of activities to keep us busy.

This year, we couldn't think of a place we wanted to go, so we stayed home.

I had always enjoyed the woods behind my house that ran

down a long slope. The terrain was so rugged, no one could build on that seventeen acres. I called it *my woods*. Our three children grew up playing back there, climbing trees and building forts among the rocks.

That January, I looked out and saw a big, yellow machine, which I hadn't noticed until the trees lost their leaves. Someone was clearing that land! A couple bought the entire seventeen acres, and the best place for their three-story house was directly behind ours.

I felt sick. I wanted to run away or cry. Thirty-five years of seeing my woods vanished, to have them replaced by a three-story house with other outbuildings. It was too much. Next, a fence was raised, and white pines were planted for a screen, and the outline of our backyard changed.

We had already decided to stay home, but life became dull, and every time I looked out back, I became more depressed. For the first time, I waited for the fog, hoping it would hide the construction of the new house and the big yellow machine.

I needed a project, so I decided to paint the kitchen. Then I became allergic to the oil paint I used and fell ill.

Around that time, I received a phone call from Columbus, Georgia, from my sister, saying I had to visit her. My father, age ninety-one, was in the hospital with severe pain and pneumonia.

That was the beginning of my first trip to Georgia. I had always hated driving through Atlanta, but I had to. For some reason, it always rained when I came through, and the traffic was always horrendous.

Somehow, I made it, and I slept on a cot in Dad's room for several nights. I came home for a few days' rest, then returned when he had to undergo some risky surgery to deal with a cancer the doctors found wrapped around his spine.

I drove home up Highway 27, which was worse than the

other road, with workers repairing the road in many places. There were several detours, and I became lost. Once I found I was driving back toward Columbus. I'd been down there many times, but I was getting older, and I wasn't the best driver in the world, and I couldn't seem to get my trip planned right.

Being lost frustrated me more than anything. I felt helpless. All I could think of was to cry. I finally understood what the Bible meant by the words, *lost without Christ.* I couldn't imagine being lost for eternity.

On my third trip, I went down when Dad was sent to a hospice in Columbus. I refused to drive and took a shuttle to Atlanta, then changed to the Columbus shuttle at the Atlanta airport. The vehicles were parked side by side in the ground transportation area.

I stayed with Dad at the hospice until he died. The precious father whom the world had known for ninety-one years was now in heaven.

All the stress got to me, and I broke out with hives. My father's wife is a hairdresser, and she cut my hair while we were at the hospice without setting it. I looked pretty bizarre. My thirty-year-old nephew took me to what we called a "doc in the box," because it was Sunday, and he gave me what he called a "Forrest Gump" shot in the same part of the body where Forrest was shot in the movie.

When I left, my nephew looked at my hospice haircut, red welts, and remembered my shot, then said, "Gee, Aunt Margie, I hope this isn't contagious."

As I rounded the curves driving up our mountain from the shuttle station, I saw green sprigs in a few places. There were even a few buds on the forsythia, or something yellow, besides the machinery I'd become accustomed to viewing.

Finally, on January 31, the sun came out. January was over.

Friends and Family

Mary Jane, Molly, Liz, and Lois had been friends for years. No one could remember how they met—they knew only that they'd known each other for thirty-five years—and the four women couldn't have been more different.

Mary Jane came from the deep South in Alabama, and she still had her natural Southern drawl. It was soft and sweet, but she could lay it on thick if she wanted to show off or was angry. She didn't mind being teased about being from Dixie. In fact, she was proud of it. However, she resented the implication that people from other parts of the country made when they assumed all Southerners were from the backwoods and had no education. Mary Jane read a lot, taught *English as a Second Language*, and wrote after her husband retired. She was also an excellent Bible teacher and speaker.

Molly, from New York City, married a man who ran a publishing company. They eventually retired in the South to be near their children. She was very conservative and proper and did a lot of entertaining for her husband's clients, and, later, his friends. He was a golfer.

Liz came from the Midwest. Her husband was transferred to the South to head a manufacturing company. She was definitely unconventional. She wore no makeup, allowed her hair to be completely natural, and let it fall straight with bangs. She was extremely bright and witty. Because she loved the arts, she volunteered to be a docent at the local museum.

Lois was the oldest of the four, but she was, by far, the most active. She loved the outdoors and hiked a lot, taking nearby trails, and she often went canoeing down the rapids of the Ocoee River. Her husband had been transferred to the South many years earlier, and, when he died, she stayed, because she had very little family elsewhere.

Mary Jane's husband was the last of the Southern gentlemen. He strongly believed a woman should be a *keeper at home* as the Bible called it, and the man was the head of the house. He never missed a day in Sunday school as a child, mostly because of his Aunt Lala. She sat him on the porch swing with her and taught him Bible verses, giving him a dime for each one he learned. She was also his Sunday school teacher. He finally landed a job with a large corporation, attended night school, and quickly climbed the corporate ladder. He was a self-educated, self-made man.

All four ladies were in their seventies, and their common interest was bridge. They had played together for over twenty years. They all lived in a little town in the Tennessee mountains for the past thirty-five years. Molly reared two children, Mary Jane had three, Liz survived four, and Lois had none.

Sometimes, they took trips together. Once they went overseas, but mostly, they took bus trips to nearby scenic places. Usually, only three went, because Mary Jane's husband wasn't too keen on her going off without him. However, she still had the privilege of her younger days of accompanying him on company trips, so she'd been to many places. They married at nineteen, and Mary Jane went from her daddy's home to her husband's and had never lived alone like the other three women.

The ladies always met for birthdays. On one dreary, foggy day in January, Molly, Liz, and Lois gathered to plan a birthday outing for Mary Jane. Each called Mary Jane several times, but they never received an answer, even from her answering machine, which wasn't normal. Mary Jane was letting her hair become gray, and she often wore wide-brimmed hats or scarves to hide the line of outgoing color and incoming gray. Her hair would someday be a beautiful white, but at the moment, it looked awful. She'd also had recent eye surgery, and she wore large, black sunglasses to hide her eyes.

"Maybe she's around, and we just don't recognize her," Molly said. "Where would her husband be? When he's home, he always answers, and he asks who's calling."

The other women smiled at that.

"Perhaps she went to visit her sister in Georgia," Liz commented.

"No," Lois said. "She always tells me when she's leaving town."

They sat quietly for a few moments, thinking and sipping tea as fog rolled in.

"You know," Molly said, "she's never been anywhere on her own. I'll bet she ran away."

"Could be," Liz replied. "She always threatened to do that, but I thought she was kidding."

"Maybe her children would know," Lois suggested.

"I doubt it," Liz said. "She doesn't report to them."

"She hates January, you know," Molly said. "Something

bad always happens to her in that month, remember? Do you think she's depressed?"

All three finished their tea while watching the fog become thicker by the moment.

Mary Jane walked along a deserted mountainside as the early morning's last bit of unmelted snow sparkled on the grass below her feet. From a certain viewpoint, she could see God's beautiful creation for miles. Mountains, trees, streams, and heavy undergrowth were sprinkled with the last bits of melting snow and ice.

The severe storm did a lot of damage. Trees were bent, twigs were broken, and some power lines were down. Fog was rolling in, making uneven patches in the skyline.

One false step, she thought, *and I'd be down this cliff, and no one would ever find me. No one knows where I am—or why.*

The surrounding campus was deserted, because the students hadn't yet returned from the Christmas holiday. A conference had just departed, making a dirty little apartment available at a very low price. It included a bed, small stove and refrigerator, and nothing else. The phone was at the end of the hall, so an emergency call from her room wasn't possible.

At some distance away on the campus, overlooking the cliff, was a huge cross flanked by buildings that housed classrooms. It seemed like an eternity back to the time when she was last on that campus. In fact, she had been to school for only one year before she married and began her home and family.

"When you walk through a storm, keep your head high," her grandmother told her.

As a child, she spent many wonderful hours with her grandmother. She would always remember what that remarkable lady told her. As she remembered those words, she lifted her head as she walked along the edge of the cliff.

On her drive up in the wee hours of the morning, she thought of a Bible verse, so she stopped the car and pulled over. Using a flashlight, she looked up the verse.

That's what I thought, she said. *I'm trapped.*

Suddenly, two policemen approached, one on either side of the car, their hands on their guns.

"Lady, what are you doing?" one asked.

"I'm reading my Bible with this flashlight. Can't you see that?"

"Ma'am, it's four-thirty in the morning."

"I know that."

"Well, as long as you're all right...."

She closed her Bible, pulled her car back onto the road, and continued her journey.

Where were they now? Where would they be if she fell down the cliff? She wished she were like Lois and would see the challenge of hiking to the bottom. Maybe she should be like Molly, the cook and entertainer, and she could try a new recipe on the dirty stove in her room. Liz would've brought an extra blanket and gone back to the dorm to read a book about art.

She was none of those. She was Mary Jane, and she just wanted to be alone, walking and thinking.

As the sun rose, she noticed a figure coming toward her with the sun at his back. It was hard to distinguish his features, but, as he approached, she saw it was her husband.

"My word, Mary Jane," he said. "Whatever possessed you to do such a thing? Don't you have a lovely home and a car, all completely paid for? Don't you have three lovely children with nice manners and happy families? They would be worried to death if they knew you'd disappeared. Don't you have friends—what are their names?—who'd be shocked?

"You shouldn't feel threatened, because I'm away so often. My committee meetings are important to me. You must keep up your image, you know. I tried to call you when my AARP meeting ran overtime, and I had to take a later flight, but I received no answer. What happened to the answering machine? Can you guess how I knew where you'd be? I remembered all those times you asked me to bring you here to one of the bed and breakfast hotels.

"Silly idea. That's for honeymooners. Anyway, I'm here now, and I've found you. Get your things, and I'll follow you home. I'll make a nice fire, and I'd like for you to make some of your homemade soup. That would be nice on a cold, foggy evening. You'd better call your friends as soon as you're home."

Mary Jane wanted to say, "Lift up your thumb. I want out from under. Loosen up the leash. I'd like to have a little more space."

Instead, she said nothing. *Just as I thought,* she observed. *Nothing has changed, and it's only the first part of January.*

January Ghosts

I despise January! Nothing good ever happens in that month. That January was even worse. My husband finally decided to make his departure final, and I had to get away.

Years earlier, we bought a country place with a pond in the middle of the woods. We had some horses, a barn, and a rustic cabin. Although it was January and a bit cold for a vacation there, I thought a nice fire in the fireplace and some rides in the woods would help my mood. I needed to be alone.

I arrived in late afternoon, and the caretaker helped me saddle the mare for a ride. The territory was unfamiliar, as we hadn't been there in quite a while, but it was beautiful as I began riding. The sun was about to set, and its golden rays made lovely shadows through the trees.

It was strange, however, how those once-familiar woods seemed so different and uncomfortable as the sun set, and evening unrolled her ebony cloak. The day's stress usually left as the smooth cadence of hoofbeats echoed through the woods, but not that evening.

As we rounded the bend of the pond, my horse stumbled and stopped. I dismounted and lifted her foot to find a small pebble wedged there. Carefully, I used a small stick to remove it, then we resumed our ride.

Looking back, I noticed strange vapor gathering on the pond, which wasn't normal for January. *Maybe fog is on its way.* The silent mist seemed to follow us from the pond like a huge puff of smoke. If my mare slowed, so did the mist.

As I looked back, I saw the shimmering pond shining in the light of the golden moon. Suddenly, everything went dark, and I could barely see the trail. When I turned to look at the pond again, it had completely disappeared from view.

The moon was hidden behind a dark cloud. I wondered if rain was coming and wished I'd brought a flashlight and rain jacket, perhaps even a gun. When I'd left the cabin to begin my ride, it was a lovely evening.

The night suddenly gained momentum, and the darkness accelerated, even with the golden moon rising. I heard wind rustling, then stopping. The leaves under my horse's hooves were muffled in the stillness.

Suddenly, I heard a shrill, shrieking woman's voice. A slinky shadow slid past in the semidarkness.

I must be a victim of something terrible, I thought. *No one knows where I am.*

I felt deflated, devastated, and depressed. My only friend and confidant was the horse, and she had stopped again. Behind me came the sound of hoofbeats, and those didn't stop.

While the sound of my bay's hoofbeats helped relieve my stress, the new ones didn't. Dismounting, I stood breathlessly behind a large tree, my heart pounding. The wind made an eerie sound as it blew through the trees, tossing the leaves.

Suddenly, the sound stopped.

"Hi," a male voice said. "I've been keeping an eye on you. I hope you don't mind. I'm your neighbor. They sprayed the pond with pesticides today and raked up quite a few loose pebbles onto the trail around the bend. They put up a sign asking us to avoid the area for two or three days, but I guess you didn't see it. Shall I follow you until you're safely back at the barn?"

"No, thanks. I can make it now."

When I opened my eyes, I lay on a strange couch with two strangers looking down at me.

"You must've fainted," the man said. "You fell to the ground with your horse standing nearby, right near the bend of the pond. We're your new neighbors, so we brought you to our house. We weren't certain where you lived."

His wife brought tea and cheese crackers. It was dark out, and the moon was gone. "We gave your horse a snack. She's tied outside with ours."

When I awoke in my bed, I wasn't sure if it really happened, or if I had dreamed it. I reclined alone in my retreat. My heart raced, and I couldn't lie still. It was daylight, and the shimmering sun shone slightly through the trees.

At the rear of the house, I saw something shiny that someone had dropped. It was a silver snap, sparkling in the sunshine, attached to a slender black strap that might've come from a tape recorder.

Not a woman at all I heard last night, I thought. *It was a man using a woman's voice on a tape recorder. Now I know who's trying to frighten me. My worst enemy was once my best friend and husband. He's lurking out here, longing to get me. Where will I be willing to wander and wait? Where will I find a weapon?*

I opened my hand and found myself clutching the pebble I took from my horse's hoof.

Wondering, worrying, and wishing it hadn't happened, I sat frozen on the back steps. After all, it was still January.

Office at Home

My husband has been retired for fourteen years. Once I was at a ladies' tea party, and one of the women said, "My husband has been retired for thirty years."

We gasped.

My husband took one of the spare rooms on the lower level of our tri-level house and began some part-time work to help people in his field. Mostly, he worked for free, but he received many calls due to his expertise with mortgage lending and joint venturing in shopping centers and other real estate. He had a wide range of friends from across the country, plus an amazing memory for transactions he once handled.

I had a great time decorating the office for him. We removed the bedroom furniture and replaced it with a large, office-sized roll-topped desk that housed a computer, and an elegant leather recliner. A dark-green carpet enhanced the room.

On that particular day in early January, when life was dull after the holidays, my husband received a call from Henry, a man he met years earlier while speaking at a seminar and hadn't seen since.

"I'm in a panic," Henry said. "We can't locate the original ground lease for the shopping center I'm working on, and we're supposed to close immediately. Can you help?"

Blessed with an amazing memory for business, although he always forgot our children's and grandchildren's birthdays and dental appointments, my husband immediately said, "Call Joe."

"I don't know him. Would you handle it, please?"

My husband sent messages via E-mail and the telephone. Within a few days, he located the original, twenty-year-old lease that a team of men hadn't been able to find.

"My God," Henry said. "You sure saved my ass."

Having been reared as a Southern, Christian lady, I don't normally use such language, but that is a direct quote and seems appropriate. With Henry's ass saved, the closing was covered, and life returned to normal—until the next phone call.

"Do you remember the deal you worked on in Atlanta, where the old building was converted to office space?" an Atlanta businessman asked my husband. "I know your company has the information on that, and I want to refinance. It took place years ago. That part of the city has deteriorated. Can you get them to refinance it so I can restore the building?"

Once again, my husband rummaged in the old papers in his closet, and he started sending E-mails again. That deal took a couple of trips to Atlanta, and I honestly think my husband was the only one who remembered what was needed, or could have gotten that deal through. There is a lot to be said for older gentlemen who've retired.

The following week, a local business associate called and said, "We want you as an expert witness in our court case involving the Market Shopping Center. You remember that one. I'll bring over the depositions."

When the man arrived, he handed my husband a box of paper the thickness of a phone book. "We'll pay you, of course."

My husband was overwhelmed. He closed his office door and read those papers for weeks. Finally, his friend called back and said, "We've settled out of court. Send us your bill."

My husband stacked the papers, left the door open on his office, and smiled. At least that January wasn't dull for him.

"Boy," he said, "I'm sure glad to be out of that rat race." He stretched out on the sofa by the fire.

"Remember," I said, "it's almost our oldest son's birthday, and we need to plan something."

"Uh-huh." He began dozing.

Seventy-Something

Being in your seventies is wonderful, Lucy thought, although she hadn't thought that way at first. She passed through every decade of her life without flinching, but, when she reached seventy, something was different.

For one thing, her body began giving her trouble. She had a different doctor for every body part. Her energy level slacked off, and her interests changed. Her mother died twenty years earlier at the age of sixty-seven, leaving Lucy without a role model for her new decade.

Her husband was her age, and she noticed a definite change in him, too. He no longer cared about golf, didn't want to go out to eat, and wasn't much interested in company or taking trips.

On Lucy's birthday in January, when Lucy turned seventy, she didn't feel much like celebrating.

It was remarkable how much time was spent making doctor's appointments, waiting in their offices, going in for tests, and doing it all over again with her husband. One day, after an exasperating two hours waiting in a doctor's office for a follow-up visit, she announced to him that she charged $25 dollars an hour waiting that long. He was so startled, he made her future appointments first on his list.

That was when she discovered she could be assertive. Usually, it worked.

Then there was the time she was told that one of her doctors couldn't possibly see her, because she came in without an appointment. She was also told that her husband, who accompanied her, couldn't be with her during the visit. She sat patiently after announcing that the doctor had told her to return if she had a problem, and assured the nurse he would see her immediately.

When there was a lull, Lucy took her husband's hand, led him around the receptionist's desk, and entered the inner office. The doctor was pleased to see them, the check-up took only five minutes, and they left with a prescription suitable for both.

Lucy realized that older women had some clout after all.

I also discovered, she thought, *that I can now decline bridal invitations for teas. I can even skip the wedding. I can say, "No thank you," to filling in at bridge. I can have other plans when fund-raising luncheons come up, and I can say, "I'm sorry, but we are retired and can't contribute at this time," to telemarketers who call at dinnertime. I can even drink wine in public!*

Lucy believed God was preparing her for a major change in her life, so she reclined in her favorite chair and pondered the idea. She thought of things she could do now she couldn't have done before.

I can sit by the fire in my flannel pajamas and robe with my rabbit-fur slippers, and I can declare it's Robe Day and stay in my robe all day if I want.

When ice and snowstorms come, I can sit by my window and

watch my neighbors trying to get out of their driveways. I can stay inside my air-conditioned house when it's ninety-eight outside. I can nap whenever I choose, or I can read a book undisturbed. I don't have to watch TV if I don't want to. I can leave my bed unmade. I can avoid shopping centers and crowds.

I haven't bought wrapping paper in years. Checks are fine for gifts. I can skip all the elaborate Christmas decorations and stay home on New Year's Eve.

I can go to church in my flat shoes that lace up and wear a pants suit. If I don't want to go to the post office or grocery store, I can go tomorrow. I can get up any time I wish and work on my computer or send E-mail. I no longer have to arrange my day to match the school-bus schedule. I've been there and done that.

Younger people open doors for me. I can get a wheelchair in large, busy airports. I can wear a winter shawl in an air-conditioned building, and no one cares.

I've let the fake color grow from my hair, and it's snow white in front. Someone once told me, "You look older." I replied, "I am." In the Bible, I read "White hair is a crown of glory and is seen most among the godly" (Proverbs 16:31-33).

In short, I've found a whole new life! I'm no longer known as "her daughter, his wife," or "their mother." I'm Lucy. I have my own identity!

Another birthday's coming up, and it's January. It is great to be in my seventies!